Often I Am Happy

Jens Christian Grøndahl

TRANSLATED BY THE AUTHOR

LARGE
PRINT

First published in Great Britain 2017
by
Picador
an imprint of Pan Macmillan

First Isis Edition
published 2018
by arrangement with
Pan Macmillan

A catalogue record for this book is available
from the British Library.

ISBN 978–1–78541–572–2 (hb)
ISBN 978–1–78541–578–4 (pb)

Published by
F. A. Thorpe (Publishing)
Anstey, Leicestershire

Set by Words & Graphics Ltd.
Anstey, Leicestershire
Printed and bound in Great Britain by
T. J. International Ltd., Padstow, Cornwall

This book is printed on acid-free paper

OFTEN I AM HAPPY

When Ellinor addresses her best friend Anna, she does not expect a reply. Anna has been dead for forty years, killed in a skiing accident that claimed Henning's husband and Anna's lover. Ellinor tells her friend that Georg has died — Georg who was once Anna's, but whom Ellinor came to love in her place, and whom she came to care for, along with Anna's two infant sons. Yet, after Georg's death, Ellinor finds herself able to cut the ties of her assumed life with surprising ease. Returning to the area of Copenhagen where she grew up, Ellinor finds herself addressing her own history: her marriage to Henning, their seemingly charmed friendship with the newlywed Anna and Georg, right back to her own mother's story — one of loss and heartbreaking pride.

Often I am happy and yet I want to cry;
For no heart fully shares my joy.
Often I am sorrowful yet have to laugh,
That no one shall my fearful tear behold.

— B. S. INGEMANN

Now your husband is also dead, Anna. Your husband, our husband. I would have liked him to lie next to you, but you have neighbors, a lawyer and a lady who was buried a couple of years ago. The lawyer had been around for a long time when you joined them. I found a vacant plot for Georg on the next row; the back of his stone is visible from your grave. I opted for limestone, although the stonemason said it wouldn't be weather-proof. So what? I don't like granite. The twins would have liked granite — on this point they agreed for once. Granite is too heavy, and our Georg had been complaining about this weight on his chest. We should have taken it more seriously, but he shrugged it off. At first he moaned, and when you wanted to share his concern you were brushed aside. Georg was like that.

He collapsed in the shower. I knew right away that something was wrong, or only now I think I knew it. He groaned and it felt anomalous to maneuver his heavy, wet body. He was still conscious as I got him to bed. When the ambulance came, it was all over. He looked like himself, older but still nice enough. His belly was less protruding when he was lying on his back. You never saw him that way, but seventy-eight is nothing, really, don't you agree? Or seventy, for that matter. It could have been you who found him on the tiles under the jet of hot water. Normally, it would have been you. Can you say that? He always stayed out there for so long. He might easily have remained standing if his coronary artery had not burst. It could have been your life continuing just like that. Where would I have been, in your life? Where would I have been in mine? I caressed him as we were waiting for the ambulance to come, but I don't know if he felt anything. At some point as I sat with him, there was no longer anything to feel. I realized it later. He could not feel my touch, as if I were the one who was suddenly absent. His absence felt like a lump growing inside me, making me suffocate. I never felt so alone. One is used to reality responding or just resounding with whatever one thinks or feels. Death shuts up the living; the real is our enemy in the long run.

The day after the funeral, I biked to the cemetery again. I took a couple of the sprays and put them in front of your headstone. Otherwise, I have brought you flowers only when it was your birthday. The first years I came quite often, mostly alone. Georg didn't like to come along, and in the end I'd stopped telling him that I had been at your grave. At that time, it had been ages since I'd stopped asking him why he wouldn't come. I don't think he ever forgave you completely, but even that he probably wouldn't have wanted to admit, had I asked him. I might have construed his answer in the sense that I had not been fully capable of filling your place. He was so considerate, and I think he had come to be really fond of me. The years passed, mind you, and in the end we belonged together, simply because we lived side by side. We underestimate the power of habit while we're young, and we underestimate the *grace* of it. Strange word, but there it is.

For me it was never a question of forgiveness once you were gone. It doesn't make sense to stand there forgiving or not forgiving a stone, be it limestone or granite. Your life, any life, is reduced to a handful of facts when it ends. It was. This and that happened, and we can make of it what we like. You went to bed with your best friend's husband and allowed him to drag you to your death. Of course, none of you had counted on that. To begin with, I asked myself what you had expected. Would you have suggested that we simply swap? Those things happen.

At the time, when I was still pondering my unanswered questions, I reached the conclusion that you probably had not expected anything at all. It can be difficult, if one is not in love oneself, to imagine the extent to which lovers are oblivious of the future or other people. They are immersed in their bliss, and it spreads around them in all directions. Its moment will not let itself be replaced by the next or yet another. They are amply occupied with the face and body of the other, and with the strange jealousy that even I remember vaguely, although it is a long time since I fell in love. You are jealous of neither rivals nor the thought of rivals — before that kind of jealousy comes another, and only the man you love is concerned. You are jealous of his body, because it is closer than you will ever get to his thoughts.

No, you hadn't thought of anything in particular concerning me or Georg, and certainly not that I would one day stand at your grave together with your husband and your twin boys. You see, there was just one grave to stand at. Throughout the years, I have been haunted from time to time by the same misplaced whim of mine. What if Henning is still alive somewhere? One's head cannot grasp the idea that people may just disappear; it is like eternity. Impossible to imagine. But there we were, Georg, the twins, and I. Of course I didn't want him at all for the first long stretch of time.

They've been down on me lately, the twins. I am probably being too abrupt, too determined. It is possible that I am a little callous without knowing myself, but on the other hand, I do find them terribly sentimental. I am of course respectful of their mourning; I mourn their father myself. Why do I feel the need to say so? I think I sense a certain doubtfulness in them. I just cannot see why I should sit like some custodian in their childhood home now that Georg is gone. Look at the furniture, watch over the position of chairs and tables in the rooms, hunt the dust. I could of course have waited for a year, let the anniversary of his death pass, and then make my decision, but why? None of them intend to move in, and Georg remains as dead after three weeks as he will be a year from now. I didn't weep at the funeral; maybe that's why they question my feelings. I had finished weeping. I wept all night when I came back from the

4

hospital, until I fell asleep on the couch without having lit a single lamp. I couldn't go to bed, but it wasn't because of him. It wasn't that he had just died in the same bed, and the proof is, I didn't change the sheets for several weeks. I slept in them until I no longer felt his smell. That is one thing I would have liked to talk to you about, Georg's smell. How can you know someone so well without having words to describe how they smell? His smell is a fact in my remembrance, and it stays there, undescribed. It was, and is no longer but as a speechless recollection.

But they seem to think that I am tough, your sons. Why can't they just think that I am in shock? Shouldn't we just say that I am in shock, Anna? Trouble is, I can't really say it myself. Who in shock will find the poise to look up the phone number of a real estate agent? Their problem is that I called the agent and put the house on the market before the attorney had gotten around to sending an appraiser. The order of factors, you know, was never my strong point. Isn't it supposed to be arbitrary? Who loved this or that man first. Love was, that is the bottom line, to use one of Stefan's favorite expressions. It is strange how different they have become, Stefan and Morten. One wouldn't think that they are twins.

Love was. Is it no longer? Yes, it is; it does not die with the man, but for how long will it flutter by itself, reach out in the empty rooms for the grains of dust in a shaft of sunlight? When does it become the memory of a feeling, no longer the feeling itself? I loved you, Anna, and my love was greater than my rage. None of us could have known that. I came to love Georg in your place, and I wouldn't have thought so, either, but to live on in the silent rooms where he is absent? For some reason it seems unthinkable, and I would like to understand why.

Until I do, the bottom line is that I attended a meeting yesterday at the executor's office, and I felt your sons' pent-up — what should I call it? Indignation? Disappointment? In any case, it was an embarrassing cocktail of emotions seeping through and around the attorney's long, polished table. A woman in tight slacks and a fitted jacket, about their age, with corporate spectacles before her painted eyes. I think Morten found her sexy. I suspect that he has a weakness, since he never became really bourgeois himself, for exactly that sort of chilled, self-relying femininity. Stefan, for his part, did not let himself be affected; as usual he was transparency and straightness impersonated, every bit the banker. One of your sons became an investment manager, Anna, another thing I don't believe you would have imagined. The other one is an art historian, which you would probably have found less remote. The vigilant eyes of the executor may have made him think of *Girl with a Pearl Earring*. I myself was falling into a reverie when I was called to order. I had put the house up for sale? It was the attorney asking, and you know what it's like when something is ascertained by way of a question. No, of course you don't know that anymore; you know nothing, and you have no ears to hear any of this. Your pretty ears with rosy earlobes are no longer.

It is absurd of me to address you, but if I don't, it will be as if I, too, were just another fact, like a stone, nothing more. As if what I see before my mind's eye could not resound just a little with what I think and feel. And I have seen you for forty years, Anna. You stopped there, not one day older. You have really fallen behind. But my mouth ran dry, and I already felt guilty before I had been accused of anything. I said I wanted to give them their dues, but I stopped when Stefan sent me a look. He leaned forward, and I saw five small misty spots dwindle and then disappear where his fingertips had rested on the glossy tabletop. He raised one hand, as if to allay the anger that we were not at any price supposed to recognize by his tone. We might have talked about it; of course I could stay in my home for as long as I wished, and if it was a question of money . . . We could always talk about it, he repeated, and he turned to Morten, who just nodded.

The attorney said something about undivided possession, and I thought about our bed at home, how unaccustomed I still was, at night, to the undivided stillness. The linen, the pillowcases, the finely woven cotton. It was time to change. For a few endless, lonely seconds it felt again as if I were swelling inside to the point of bursting, compact and breathless, and I had to clutch the armrest. It comes when I least expect it. It would be glossing over to say that I am in mourning when it is mourning that fills me up, that shapeless lump, growing unrestrainedly. It drives me out of myself, making me gasp, and nobody will ever understand before they themselves lose someone dear

7

to them and feel the pressure. The shapeless, rising mass of grief. Yes, it is true that one is no longer oneself.

I looked stiffly at the attorney and forced myself not to blink as I said that it was no longer relevant. I told them that I had already found myself another place to live, and that I was moving out at the end of the month. I could hear the South Americans on their panpipes down at the city hall square, playing "El Condor Pasa." I don't know how long we just sat, as motionless and silent as in the chapel three weeks ago when we were waiting for the end to commence.

In the summer, Georg and I used to take our bikes, if it wasn't raining, when we were going over to Stefan and Mie's place. It wasn't as if he never got any exercise. Their house is on the other side of the bog and the riding school, and you have to get off and wheel part of the way. A shady dip of wild greenery in the midst of the otherwise regular neighborhood. When I was on my own, I liked to stop and look at the horses in the pen. The lines of a horse's body, and the skin's way of reflecting the sunlight, have always made me happier than such a sight is likely to add up to.

Of course, Stefan and Mie's house is bigger than ours, and theirs is a better street. I am stating it as a matter of course since everyone has always assumed, for as long as I have lived, that things can only move forward and up. An investment manager earns more than an insurance man, and even Georg seemed to find it appropriate. That is one field where the order of

8

factors is not arbitrary. Rich, richer; that makes sense. The reverse hardly does, but Stefan and Mie wouldn't even consider this, taking their success for granted. Meaning that they take it in their stride. We are different, those of us who were born right after the war. A reminder was sewn with tiny stitches into our frontal lobes: *Never again poor*. Even so, you are allowed to wonder that the abundance of money, now that they have achieved it, should be the purpose of their lives, and "the market" their religion. Yes, I have become a communist in my old age — I am sorry. I am the last communist in Europe. I cannot comprehend that the rich are unable to free themselves from their wealth. Mind you, Mie has to go to the bakery in their Range Rover, just to make sure that people in their neighborhood know that she has one.

I could not understand why they would settle at such a short distance from Georg and myself. If I had been in their shoes, I would have bought a house at the opposite end of the city. Georg was overcome with joy, that is, to begin with, since we didn't get to see them more often for that; and he looked at me in sincere astonishment when I told him what a woman had said to me at the swimming pool. It's the wife's family that gets to be in the good books, she said, and they are the ones whom the husband becomes attached to. It held true in Stefan and Mie's case, and I even think that the house bargain was a semiconscious way, on her part, to compensate in advance. We have been close only in the geographic sense. And I had even decided to be a nice mother-in-law when Stefan came to tell us that she was the one. I have known Mie for seventeen years without ever exchanging anything but truisms. It's not that I dislike her, and I don't think that she has anything against me in any direct way, but in her mind she has never left home. Her parents are still king and queen, and she calls them several times a day. She couldn't even propose a toast to her husband on his fortieth birthday without consulting them first.

I know, Anna, that I am getting carried away. Anyway, it's not my business. You would have been better at it, and you wouldn't have liked to hear what I'm saying, but it can't be helped. As I was riding over to their place yesterday evening, I was already aware that this would be the last time — apart, of course, from the birthdays and confirmations and Christmas Eves that no one is exempted from. It's not because Mie submits to her parents in everything, or because they're being so stuck-up and plebeian. Mind you, I know what I'm talking about, coming from the lower classes myself. But why do you think that Eliot and Franca both stutter? They are your grandchildren; Anna, that's how they're called. Stefan has never wanted to listen when I've tried to talk to him about it. His children don't stutter. They just don't know how to complete a sentence without stumbling over the words for fear of what Mom will say, and Mom has a whole lot to say. She knows best, and they are so intimate, she and the kids. According to her, there is nothing they can't talk about. Franca was breast-fed until she was four, and at age fourteen she still follows her mother

10

like a shadow. Sometimes you can hear them giggling together in the master bedroom.

Mie was in full swing at the kitchen table when I entered. I was allowed to kiss her cheeks as she spread her arms, durum dough between her fingers, making them look webbed. The pizzas must be homemade, of course. Then she remembered that, after all, it was only the third time I'd come alone, and she washed her hands in a hurry. I hesitated a little too long before I surrendered to her hug. She is all skin and bones now; a couple of years ago she looked like the cartoon character Obelix, but then she decided to become thin. Everything is a decision to Mie, a plan. She traverses the municipality every morning in her sneakers, and if Stefan asks her if she'd like a glass of wine, she says that she'd rather save the calories for something else. It was Stefan who came to the door as usual. When her parents arrived she flew out to meet them on the garden walk. Am I being petty? Yes, I am, but it's the family, Anna. It makes us small if we measure ourselves by its yardstick only. You've got to get away. Do you remember how busy we were to get going?

The first time on my own. It was like playing in a movie, the first time I ran up a new flight of stairs, locked myself in, and stepped through an unfamiliar corridor and through my very own door. I rented a room with a single woman on Søndre Fasanvej. I thought it was classy, and it was, sort of, when you came from Amerikavej. My mother couldn't understand that I was moving from one single woman to the other just because one of them happened to be my parent. I am eighteen, I answered brusquely, and she said no more. I believe that she hid her relief at no longer having me around in her one-and-a-half-room apartment, but she must also have been worried at the prospect of having to pay the rent and daily expenses all by herself. Pinch and scrape, turn every penny. I worked in a shop and took evening classes. You and I still hadn't met; I was alone in the world, that's how it felt, even if it was just a mere fifteen minutes from Frederiksberg to Vesterbro. It was still home but not a place I wished to go more often than I had to. We got along all right, my mother and I, but it was so silent between us once we'd finished telling each other what had happened since last time.

I didn't go out much, couldn't afford it. Anyway, I was happy to spend the evenings in my room, reading or listening to the radio. I turned it down so as not to disturb my landlady. Freedom was never more boundless than in my rented room on Søndre Fasanvej in the autumn of '63. On Sundays I went to the national museum of art, mostly because I didn't know what else to do with myself. I had never looked at paintings, but the painters became my friends, especially the ones who painted something I knew, even if it was half a century ago. Fishermen and peasants, people in the streets, or just the forests and furrows out in the country, the view over an undulating meadow or a vegetable garden. I thought I could hear the wind in the treetops and a clock's gravitating weights as I stood in a museum hall and forgot myself. It never entered my mind if it was cultured or in good taste to look at paintings — I just liked it. I think that was how Morten got on the track, and now there isn't a thing he can't tell you about artists, be they Renaissance or Baroque. I remember the first time I took him to Glyptoteket. He stood a long time before Manet's *Absinthe Drinker* until he asked if the man's left leg was made of rubber. He was right to ask, if you look more closely.

Morten was busy as usual pleasing Mie and being the helpful, familiar guest. He can be quite oily in an unbecoming way, especially when he falls over his feet to submit himself. At times he will even change his mind in the middle of a sentence, just to suit her. And he used to be so critical and quibbling, back home in his left-wing row house. He had been late as usual. He, too, has had to get used to showing up alone with Thea. Franca was visibly relieved at having her cousin's ear to whisper in. It was Morten's turn to have her. Before Christmas, he had believed that he was in love with a colleague from his faculty, but when Easter approached she wasn't ready after all to leave her husband. In the meantime, Morten had been ousted at full blast. Maybe he was truly in love, and maybe this was how it had to be, but it is no longer relevant to ask. There was what was, and there is what is. His ex is called Masja, but what do all these names mean to you? Life went on without you; the years have passed like an express train, its windows full of new faces. I am not even sure that you would recognize your boys. They had only just started in the first grade. Had you even begun to imagine what their adult lives would look like?

13

You would have no reason to be anything but satisfied if you could see Stefan and Mie's home. Everything is black and white, and they've demolished the walls on the ground floor to make room for the kitchen/living room. It is reminiscent of the control room in a power station, and we may choose between dispersing ourselves along half a mile of dinner table or disappearing into one of the sofas, each the size of a minibus. Between them is a coffee table made of driftwood, with a glass plate on top where photos of the kids with or without their parents are lined up, safely framed in silver. There are pictures of Mie's parents, too. She is especially proud of the driftwood; she says it has soul, and I bet she's right. Still, something about the household disgusts me. I couldn't miss how Eliot and Franca were sprawling on each of their sofas when I arrived, like lethargic seals basking in the sun, while the Filipino au pair laid the table. The children didn't know how to deal with my widowhood, and Eliot was speaking frenziedly about an upcoming high school trip to Scotland. He will probably return in a kilt. He is a handsome fellow, a bit of a dreamer like his uncle. I don't think Stefan is quite at ease with his son's reading poems rather than playing soccer and kissing girls. Mie told her brother-in-law about a sofa she thought that he ought to buy. Everyone must have a sofa; there's no home without it. She likes to assist him in his new life as a single with joint custody, but I feel how she is seized with panic and compassion because he has had to move into an apartment. Three rooms on the wrong side of the railroad tracks. I've heard her console him with the fact that, after all, he hasn't left the municipality.

It already felt as if our lives had closed again over the void left by Georg. The cavity was still there, under the surface, but when the others remembered it they became remorseful or polite, or both. Then they would look at me and lower their voices dutifully, and I would sense their expectancy without having any clear idea of what it was they expected. I couldn't grasp whether it was grief that made them awkward, or shyness when faced with the grief of another, myself in this case, or if it was something completely different that sneaked up on us in Georg's absence. Stefan made a point of taking it like a man, and he spoke about his father in anything but sloppy terms. What Georg had said or done on this or that occasion. He did say "Dad," but more as if that happened to be the name Georg had been given as a baby. We could even talk about what he was like, and smile in a healthy, loving way. How he always had to walk back and pull the door handle, although he well knew that he had locked it — that sort of detail from a person's doings. I thought we talked about him the way one would talk about someone with a handicap, very considerately. It dawned on me how the dead are counted as losers. Too bad Georg couldn't be here! That was the bottom line, beneath our devoutness.

I was reminded of something I hadn't wanted to see for years, and that I had been cowardly enough to deny whenever Georg hinted at it. Eventually, your sons were no longer that attached to their father, Anna. I suppose you can't expect all sons to be. I think they found him remote, although you and I know that he was just being shy. Suddenly, I felt alienated from your children. Throughout their childhood, I tried to treat them as if they were my own. As I saw them grow, I myself grew into the role. For ten years, nobody was closer to them than I was, apart from Georg, and sometimes I was the one they confided in. I have put iodine on their knees, I have blown up in front of them, and I have put a hand on their slight boy shoulders when they were low. I have taught them to look people in the eyes when they say hello, and I have taught them the zodiac. Love grows from that, while you are engrossed in all manner of things. Shortly after I'd moved in, I asked Georg if he hadn't had a shock when he learned that there were two rather than just one. Had he not feared being unable to love both of them equally? He smiled and shook his head. "Love just redoubles," he said. I thought about it for a long time. If he was right, then your boys' love might also sprout again.

I had come to love them, and in time they answered my love, but I haven't always found it that easy to love the grown men who've come out of it. I realized as much when I heard them exchange anecdotes about Georg. As I sat there attending their cozy mourning session, I became aware that my love for them is something that was. It is the recollection of a feeling, not the feeling itself. As long as Georg was alive I could repress this knowledge, busy delivering where he had failed because of his shyness. Closeness, involvement, laughter — I had delivered all of that. Now I just sat.

I had been sitting like that often when we visited Stefan and his family. They could easily fill up their gigantic house with themselves and whatever occupied them, stories from school and their jobs, plans for new acquisitions or exotic vacations. They always had so much going on among themselves, and I think that Georg sometimes felt the same as I did. It would have been too much to say that we were dispensable, but we somehow overflowed, if you know what I mean. They were brimming with themselves, Stefan, Mie, and the kids, and sometimes they would seem genuinely surprised to discover that we were there, too. As when Stefan suddenly turned to me. I knew right away what he was going to say. I'd had a feeling the whole time that they must have talked about me before I came. "Ellinor, won't you tell us about your new apartment?" I had asked them myself to keep calling me by my first name, back when it was all new and sensitive, with your old friend in the bed where you should have been. Where you ought to have continued to lie. I haven't tried to take your place in that sense; I remained Ellinor to them, but we did drop "Auntie."

There was an undertow in Stefan's tone, and I know him almost as well as if he were mine. A touch of something, what should I call it? Of course, sadism is way too strong, I know that. Mie came to my rescue. She said that she could well understand why I wanted to sell the house and make a fresh start. It was too big anyway, even for two. Her little declaration of support was an unintentional admission that they had talked more than a bit; otherwise, she wouldn't have found it

17

necessary to step between Stefan and me with her conciliatory remark. "Have I said that I don't understand?" Stefan smiled in the willful way that can make him seem almost intimidating. Georg and I had actually talked of selling and finding an apartment in the city center, but Stefan must have forgotten about it. "We were just a little surprised, Morten and I, I must admit that." He must have felt how his words were too heavy and sharp. "Right, Morten?" His brother cast a sidelong glance at his sister-in-law before he cleared his throat. "Well, I also understand if you wish to . . . I mean, life must go on . . ." I could see that he was embarrassed at the cliché, but I felt warm inside anyway, because he wouldn't let himself be bullied to enlist just like that.

"I bought an apartment on Amerikavej," I said and looked the boys in the eyes for a moment. The boys, I say. Stefan has been bald for the past ten years, and Morten has been wearing multifocal glasses for just as long. They knew already; it was purely pro forma that I was updating them like this at the Sunday dinner. "Bought?" Mie said, eyes wide in a feigned sort of way. "Ellinor has some money that she doesn't . . ." I have to admit that I was annoyed by Stefan's pretentious effort to sound casual. "Which has nothing to do with your father," I said, hoping he would refrain from elaborating. Fortunately, the others didn't seem surprised. "Amerikavej, isn't that in Amager?" Morten asked. He wanted to appear as open-minded as the map of Copenhagen, where all street names are listed in their own right, without prejudice of rank.

"Vesterbro," I corrected him. "You're from Vesterbro, aren't you?" Mie's eyes went even wider, and she was all smiles. She might as well have said Harlem or Hell; *exciting*, that was the message in her exaggerated, forthcoming grimace. After all, I was proving once more, for God knows which time, that I knew well how to handle knife and fork. "Ellinor grew up on Amerikavej," Stefan said bitterly. I couldn't gather if his slightly clenched teeth were his way of lamenting my humble extraction or he wanted to gibe Mie for her haughty ignorance. After all, she and I had known each other for most of her adult life. Perhaps it was just his ownership to the piffling bit of biographical info that made him tighten his kisser in such a self-important manner. I didn't correct him. He and Morten have grown up knowing that their stepmother is a girl from the gutter.

"It's completely beyond me what you want in such a neighborhood," Stefan said. "It's no longer what it used to be, apart from the fact that it must have been motley enough as it was when you were a child. Every other day one hears about shootings and gang crime. You can't leave your house without being surrounded by junkies, prostitutes, and Muslims." Mie shook her head. I couldn't help smiling. "I suppose it's up to Ellinor if she wants to return to the neighborhood of her childhood," she began. "Of course," Stefan said, "then we can all come to visit on *Amerikavej* . . ." Mie gave him a long look. "It's not exactly a place we can send the children," he continued, more calm now. "Are you afraid that they will become kidnapped?" I tried to strike a light note. "What if they are?" Stefan looked me in the eyes. "Besides, you drive them everywhere," I said.

We all became quiet. I turned to Eliot and Franca. I felt like a traitor as I broke the silence, betraying myself as well as Georg. I seized on the first subject that came to my mind. "How was your summer?" The children got it and started speaking all at once about their grandparents in Mougins and their new infinity pool. Mie could hardly conceal her pride in her parents' capacity. Eliot told me that it looked as if one could swim straight into the ravine. "Like real yacky," Franca said. "It was übercool," Eliot said and lost himself in a long account of their summer in Alpes-Maritimes. "By the way, Grandma and Grandpa send their regards," he said and swallowed his spittle as if he thought that he had spoken about them for too long. "They were so sorry that they couldn't come to the funeral," Mie said. She stretched an arm across the table and stroked the back of my hand. She must have felt how I clenched the fork. How, Anna, how was I to explain to her that for all I cared, her parents could sail their infinity pool forever? I felt guilty because I didn't put on a timid smile and instead allowed Mie to apologize that her parents hadn't brought themselves up from Mougins to bestow their condoling presence on me. It occurred to me that Stefan's hostility might in this case have been redirected since the power balance of his marriage ruled out any criticism of his parents-in-law.

Strangely enough, the reason for my bad conscience was that for once, I didn't dissimulate. It's complicated, Anna. When did I begin to withdraw from this family

20

that should have been yours? Is it only something inside me? Is it also something about them? The feeling, after all those years, that I am not the right one after all. Didn't they notice until now? Now that Georg is no longer here to gather us with a redeeming touch? When did I become a stranger again? Was I one all along?

I missed him as I was riding home on my bike. I miss him all the time, but it is something different that I miss about him at different times. His body next to me in bed, the sound of his steps, the familiar timbre of his voice in the familiar rooms. Without him, they're just somewhere. His way of sighing, which wasn't an expression of fatigue or despair but only, how to put it, a pneumatic effect of his composure. The sound of one man's being in the world. A man I loved. In the dusk, on the path through the bog, I missed having him to talk with, or maybe just that he would be there, listening. To know that he was there in the semi-darkness, within earshot, and hearing me, even if he didn't answer. His bashful nature would have kept him from responding immediately, except that he might well have been upset by what I said, without wanting to admit it to me or to himself, for that matter.

In September the days are shorter already, especially on a narrow path canopied by trees. Do you recall September? Does September make any sense in the place where you don't hear me, like Georg wasn't hearing what I wasn't saying, for the very same reason? It had been raining that morning, and the black path was blacker still, but now you couldn't even call it black anymore since nearly everything around me was, except for the flicker of receding violet over my head. An invisible horse snorted in the meadow. Soon it would be spending the night in a box in the stable of the riding school, fretfully scraping a hoof against a crack in the paving. Still moist, the path hissed under the tires, and the sound would have been only a trifle louder had two bikes rather than one been coasting downhill toward the bottom of the dip, producing a slightly intoxicating feeling. I thought of the tiny frogs I'd seen earlier in the evening as I was wheeling uphill in the opposite direction. Perhaps I ran one of them down, without feeling or hearing it. I hoped that they had gone to bed, and I couldn't help smiling at the picture-book idea, frogs in bed, an unknown life in the mound's interior, sheltered from all reason. Tears rose to my eyes because I felt him behind me for a second, slightly bent over, slightly stooping, with a sweater tied around his shoulders, not feeling the least bit cold even though autumn had set in beyond all measure. He had really believed that love and repetition could turn anyone into the right one.

When I met him he was yours, and I never imagined that he would become anything else. Nothing seems as limited as our imaginations, although we believe the opposite for years; but I know this much about myself: that it never occurred to me that I would sleep in the same bed as Georg. The man I was fond of had another body and a different name. I can't imagine what Henning would have looked like, just as I can envisage you only as the woman, still young, whom I last took leave of one morning in a hotel in the Dolomites. I had no reason to consider that this might be the final good-bye. Today, it also seems improbable that a young man would call himself Henning. Now, when a young man may call himself Eliot and know what an infinity pool is.

Henning was tall and dark, a bit nervous in the way he moved. He was a shipping trainee and became a head clerk shortly after, absolutely promising. Did you fall for his dark hair secretly, dark and interesting yourself in the paler Copenhagen of the 1960s? We didn't know each other yet, you and I. I still lived on Søndre Fasanvej. I didn't dare take Henning home with me when we had been out, although he pressed me. The lady I lived with had her rules, and no gentlemen in the room was rule number one. But he wanted me, and I was fascinated by his will. In my fascination, I sometimes forgot that I was its object, perhaps because I didn't quite believe it to begin with. One must be capable of wanting a great many things with a will such as his, so why me? He was what they call a handsome fellow, but of course you know all about that. I'm sorry, Anna, I didn't mean it that way. Or did I? Have I ever told you how I met him? I met him one summer's day in the crowd of bikes in front of an ice cream stand, on the way out to Bellevue. Sweet, isn't it? I had biked out there with a couple of girls from work. When we had been together a few times, I began to think that maybe we could be a couple.

Perhaps his story did it, since it resembled mine. He had no siblings and lived alone with his mother. He had been sent to a boarding school somewhere on Zeeland. He told me how he had stood at the station in a small town on Saturday mornings, waiting for the train to Copenhagen. A loudspeaker had blended with the bell at the level crossing: *Train arriving, do not pass*. He talked about the drag in his stomach when at first he heard something like a hissing in the rails, before the train finally approached between hills of rye and meadow, shoved by a glacier in the Ice Age into formations of clay and gravel nearly as wavy and winding as the clouds above on such a morning in April. He knew how to tell about it all and make it special. Do you remember? I became as fond of his words as I was of his dark, rough hair that reminded me of a horse's mane one could shake or bury one's nose in. He took me home, a sinister apartment on Kastelsvej with leathery plants where everything was very posh and threadbare. At first, I was afraid of his mother. She looked like a lady from another century in her black dress, and her handshake felt as if a huge bird had clutched me with its claws. I told them that my father had also died when I was little, and that I couldn't remember him. Fortunately, they asked no more questions, but I didn't escape introducing Henning on Amerikavej. My mother was much honored, and she had done everything she could because we were coming. I was ashamed and even more so for feeling that way.

We couldn't be alone together anywhere. To think that it was like that, Anna. It seems almost incomprehensible today, if you haven't lived through it. They must have

24

expected us to take one another sight unseen, so to speak. We went to the movies and kissed in the light of inane narratives flickering past. We were protagonists ourselves, and I'd never felt that way before, as if my life meant something. We got our chance one weekend when my landlady was visiting her sister on Funen. I've never told you this, although I meant to do it several times. When she was about to leave she turned in the doorway and said that she trusted me. I was in such a flurry that I made a curtsy and said yes, of course, and two hours later Henning rang the bell. We sat in her living room as if it were ours, as if we had a place of our own, a home. He kept pressing me; he loved me, he promised to be careful. In the end, I gave in. It was the first time, I mean for real; otherwise, we had only been fumbling. His condom burst, and of course we'd won the big one.

Henning was all remorse, and when I told him a few weeks later that I was pregnant, he wanted to marry me right away. That's how impulsive he was, but you know all about that. It was really quite decent of him, and I was still in love with him but didn't know which way to turn. He told his bosses at the shipping company that he was planning to get married, but they asked him to wait until he had completed his training and started as a clerk. He couldn't bring himself to tell them why it had to be right away. Luckily, he had a friend who'd also gotten himself into trouble and who could provide an address. It didn't go quite the way we'd hoped, or rather, it did so abundantly, but we didn't know until years later. When friends brought us along to Georg

25

and yourself for chestnuts and red wine, we still believed that one day we would have children.

Anna and Georg. You were the kind of people who are talked about. You were married already, and you had your own apartment in a modern block of yellow bricks on a leafy avenue in the suburbs. Georg had a car; you had your black hair and your Italian surname. Nobody knew that your father had been nothing but a brat from Salerno who had drifted north between the wars, escaping poverty, to take whatever he could get like so many other migrant workers after him. Nobody asked where anyone came from, and even now I've never met people like ourselves who acted as if our roots were in the future, in our dreams about it. We felt like visitors in a new era when we came to see you, white walls, light modern furniture, snap frames with art posters from Louisiana. It was interesting to think that Georg was almost eight years older than the rest of us although he didn't seem like it, apart from always being so calm. I admired you in your Jacqueline Kennedy dress; I admired your spirits and your waist and your hips. If I remember correctly, we became friends already that first evening with chestnuts and red wine and Nana Mouskouri on the record player. I was way too intense and completely forgot that Henning was with me. You had to excuse yourself several times because I talked and talked, even when you'd already turned around to step into the corridor and greet new guests and carry their coats into the bedroom where other coats were piling up on the bed. Do you remember? I wonder what we were talking about.

26

It felt as if we'd known each other always, and we soon became a close-knit quartet, Anna and Georg, Ellinor and Henning. You taught me how to make tiramisu twenty years before anyone knew what it was. You went with me to look at wedding dresses and casually let me know, during our search, that I could also take over yours, if I liked it. You must have known that we had no money, but you never made me feel like someone near the edge. On weekends, we went for a ride in Georg's Renault 4 up to Hornbaek to go for a swim, or to Gribskov to collect chanterelles. Your basket was always full; everything about you was exuberant, warm, alive. It isn't that I don't understand Henning, but I didn't notice anything.

We got married, and shortly after, an apartment became available in the block across from you and Georg. You could wave to us from your balcony when we stood in the kitchen window. We were regulars with one another, and there must have been a great many occasions when you and Henning would have been alone together by chance at your place or ours. I never gave it a thought. There were times, too, when I was alone together with Georg, but for me he was nothing but a dear, somewhat shy friend with his blotchy good nature and his steady, rustic hold on everything practical. We could always call Georg if a tap was dripping, or if we needed a visit from a power drill. He taught Henning to paint a bookcase without leaving any drips. I am not aware what Henning taught Georg, but I could tell from Georg's amused, slightly incredulous look that he found it interesting when Henning gave his imagination a free rein.

The more I got to know Henning, the better I liked him. He had been sailing a couple of times on the ships of the company, and he told me about the cities they had called at in South America. Once he had spent a week in Montevideo because the first officer had been taken to the hospital. He read to me from the diary he'd written on board. His words reminded me of the colorful Japanese paper flowers that unfold from shells when you drop them into a glass of water. He could make a name like Montevideo unfold in my thoughts as he read so that I saw everything very clearly, although I'd never been there. He had written poems before he went into shipping, and he had dreamed of seeing them published, but that was hopeless, of course, he told me with a smile. He kept saying that he loved me and that he wanted to have children with me. We tried; we tried and we tried until I pulled myself together and went to be examined and got a plain answer. He held me in his arms all night long and kept whispering that it didn't matter, and I knew that he was lying.

Life was all but taking shape. Our lonely, gray mothers became visitors to a world in which they had no share. I'd gotten myself a job in the advertisement department at *Berlingske Tidende*, and even if the wages were nothing to write home about I could at least contribute to the household. Besides, I worked short hours, and I was actually amused by the classifieds' peepholes into unknown lives where a room had to be let, a used car sold, or someone hoped to fall in love. When I was going home, I liked to look through the basement windows at the huge press, knowing that in a few hours the contact numbers of the empty room, the old car, or the lonely heart would be multiplied and spread all over the country. I've always lacked any ambition, and you kept reproaching me for it. You who gave up on the mere thought of a career when you became pregnant. This must have been half a year after I was informed that my uterus had been destroyed. I never told you. In the beginning, I was too upset about it, and later, when you were expecting, I didn't want to spoil your joy. You were always so generous, always ready to empathize, and if something made you happy, you wished the same for me. I also believe I am being honest when I say that I rejoiced without feeling jealous.

It may have helped that I didn't like what your pregnancy did to you. You became sluggish and flabby, and you developed this heiferish expression, but you were so happy. Georg also seemed happy, and he showed you with so many gestures how enthusiastic he was to see the object of his desire deformed until a house on piles walked about in place of the waist and hips of your once delightful body. I felt ashamed for thinking that way, and I told myself that I must have become sterile all the way up into my head. If I caught Henning gazing ravenously at your buxomness, I would keep staring at him until he noticed and lowered his eyes. It only made me feel even more ashamed, and something artificial came over me when I tried to be nice, until in the end I was almost sickened.

You have never been more beautiful than when we came to see you in the maternity ward and you sat in your bed with two instead of just one. You ought to have given one of them to us — Stefan or Morten, no matter who. I think it was worse for Henning than it was for me, but he probably still didn't know what the sight of you did to him. I don't believe that he started dreaming about you before you had moved because the apartment became too cramped.

The years are blurring, Anna. At a distance, they seem to be compressed, without any space, an amassed body of events and emotions devoid of any sequence. The perspective returns only as I write, and my perspective is different from yours, and Henning's. I had no inkling of what was going on the first winter your boys were big enough to be taken care of by your parents. Henning had suggested that the four of us go on a ski trip, and I remember how excited you were. I had never been skiing before, but of course I came along. I remember how you insisted that I come.

The telephone has been ringing a lot as Georg is no longer there to answer it. At our place, it was the man's job. To respond, to stand in front to meet the world. I always disliked answering the phone without knowing who it was. It frightens me a little, I don't know why, as if someone wants to hurt me. That's the good thing about cell phones, at least if it's someone I know. Not right now, is what I think when I see the name on the display, and the guilt is offset by my relief at evading the communicativeness of my surroundings. You always laughed at my fear of phones, but you also gave up on curing me of it. On the whole you never tried to reform me, and neither did Georg. I am grateful for that; it made me feel at home with both of you. You were my country, first one, then the other, and now I am stateless. To begin with, Henning would have liked to change me if he could. He never said anything, but I sensed that my breasts were too small and slanting, and I might also have had a prettier nose.

Am I being unfair? Is it only my self-hatred playing me a trick? Self-hatred is a gendered feeling: in a man it makes him a wimp; in a woman it's the natural order to feel defective. Original sin is our element, Anna; as a

Catholic you should know these things. You see, that's why God blessed us with moodiness, menstrual pain, and hot flashes with a mustache, once we get that far. Not to speak of labor, but that I was spared. And since Henning was to blame for it, he taught himself to conceal his dissatisfaction with my other flaws. He became so considerate and thoughtful after I had been molested in an illegal clinic, and his consideration left an acrid taste. I had to sugar myself to make sure that he wouldn't notice and to just forget about it, affecting cheerfulness, affecting rapture in bed, where we no longer had to be careful. Consideration distanced us from one another, I can see that now, and in the void he caught sight of you. Anna with her brown eyes and crackling voice. Original sin had bounced off; you took even the pain of being a woman with your head held high. It always passed, and you were radiant with your own soft, honey-skinned well-being.

But as I was saying, the telephone has been ringing. People won't let me sit alone. They don't want me to believe that I've become untouchable in their eyes because death has visited my house. They want me to talk about it; they want me to have closure. I am more than welcome to cry, because it allows them to show me how they endure my inconsolable sorrow. Apparently, nothing is more purifying for people's self-esteem than to place themselves at the very edge of someone else's grief and show that they are not at all dizzy. Nobody tells me that life must go on. There is room for wailing; all I have to do is let go. I felt it at the funeral, the too-long-and significant looks or, to the contrary, a feigned normalcy, as if to show me they knew very well that no words were adequate anyway. I'm not being fair, of course; what are people supposed to do with a bereaved person? They do their best, but the trouble is that when it comes to professions of sympathy, I'd rather not, whereas I am sure to be all by myself in the dead of night whenever I could use a hug. The first couple of weeks, I answered the phone out of a sense of duty and to show that I appreciated how people went out of their way to empathize. Gradually, I became better at letting it ring, and my cell hasn't been charged since Georg died. To pull the plug would feel like a decidedly hostile measure, considering the solicitude on display, but I couldn't feel obliged to plug in the charger just to make myself more accessible. There should be a limit to the officiousness of a woman in mourning.

I don't know why I answered the phone on the morning after I'd been eating homemade pizzas at Mie and Stefan's and put up with their ambivalence, not to speak of mine. It was still early, and normally nobody calls at that hour; my friends know well that I like to sleep late. I thought that it might be some research institute wishing to know about my consumer behavior, but I answered it after all. The unusual time of day must have made me curious, for all I know, but I certainly didn't expect Mie at the other end. I can't recall when she has ever called us; it was always Stefan who invited us or just wanted to know how we were. She must have been back from her jogging. I visualized her standing at the kitchen counter with the wireless.

33

Perhaps a pulse meter was still fastened to her tanned arm, her skin slightly flabby because she'd lost so much weight. I could see her ponytail and tight, neon-colored suit, a small proletarian flirt, and on one of her fingers clutching the receiver a voluminous diamond ring, a gift from Stefan on her fortieth birthday. What did she want, I thought to myself as she chatted for a start. I forgot to thank her for the evening. She suggested that we meet for coffee later in the day. It was momentous.

We met at a coffee place near the station, at the end of the leafy avenue where we once lived. It would have been to your liking, a bakery/espresso bar with stools in the window where you can sit and be on the way from one thing to the other. You died before espresso reached Denmark, and I remember how you laughed at my surprise, in the bar of the central station in Bolzano, at how tiny the cups were. You felt at home, and I enjoyed hearing you speak Italian with the barman. You also enjoyed my hearing it. A few days later it was all over, and I will never understand, Anna, how time has only made it even harder to grasp.

Mie was already waiting on a stool in the window when I came at the hour we'd arranged. She waved and seemed almost ingratiating. It's been a long journey, as they say in *X Factor*, all the way down the avenue. We started out in the cheap end, the four of us, happy just to exchange the dirty city for trees, orderliness, and a balcony of one's own. You and Georg were the first couple of our set to buy a house. You were always the first, and the house looks like its old self. I had just left it as I parked my bike outside, wondering what Mie

34

wanted. I had my misgivings and accepted a caffe latte, although I never take milk. While she was standing in line at the counter, I tried to analyze why I was on my guard. After all, I had no need to feel threatened just because she had proposed for the first time ever that we meet one-on-one. To begin with, she just wanted to know what it was like, going to bed and waking all alone, et cetera. More empathy; I was relieved. I said that it was difficult, mostly to honor her goodwill. She nodded, letting me talk, but every now and then she would allow herself a sip from her paper cup. I liked her for the little touch of self-care in the midst of her earnest compassion. She was wearing a nice buttoned dark-blue dress with a collar, and she had arranged her hair with a ribbon. I asked myself what I'd ever had against her.

"Aren't you supposed to be at your office?" I said. She said that she had a day off. I was hoping that she hadn't taken the day off for my sake. "Stefan is worried about you," she continued. I couldn't help smiling and asked if he had told her to call me. She looked at me before she said no, slightly offended. "He is mad at me for selling the house," I said. "I think you're mistaken," she said. "Don't get me wrong, you know I understand you, but why do you want to move all the way into town?" I smiled again. "You said it yourself yesterday: It's where I come from." She nodded. "But we all live out here. You could find something closer. That way, it would also be easier for the kids to come by." I kept smiling. "Look, they don't bother to come anyway."

I didn't smile in any bitter sort of way, but that's how it is. Eliot and Franca don't come by for pancakes anymore. They loved how I could turn them in the air; they loved that I always made a show of it. In their company, my joy became easier than it had been together with the twins. It made less of a difference to the next generation that we weren't really family. I felt free when I took them to the forest or they slept over. I was what they call a spry granny, but I think I know when the first chink, the first reservation, began to open between us. Eliot must have been nine, Franca seven, when Stefan and Mie came by with them one Sunday afternoon. The weather was bad, and I had given them a drawing pad each and a box of crayons so that they might entertain themselves while the grown-ups were talking. I didn't want them to watch TV just because it was raining, and it didn't take long before Franca came up to me and wanted to show me her drawing. She had drawn a princess in front of her castle, but to be honest, it wasn't more than a few hasty lines. I told her that she ought to make more of an effort. After all, I'd seen how well she could draw if she took the trouble, but suddenly, the chit started to howl and ran to her mother. "Elli doesn't like my drawing," she blubbered. At first I thought that she was complaining about her brother, but that's how they've called me. I guess it's part of the package. You see, for many years I felt that at long last I had a family. Mie got up with the squalling Franca and carried her to the sofa. I got a cold look as she murmured into the child's ear. Everyone fell silent at the table. "You criticized her," Stefan said. "You're not supposed to criticize a child." On the sofa, Franca was still sobbing into her mother's knees. I had no memory of ever seeing her like that when I was alone with the kids, touchy and moaning. "I didn't criticize her," I said, but Stefan just shook his head. "You undermine her self-worth that way," he said. It was the first time I noticed that the words coming out of his mouth weren't always his own. Perhaps I overinterpret the incident; perhaps I was the sensitive one for not being Franca's biological grandmother. In any event, I thought of it again as I sat on my stool and felt Mie's dissatisfaction with me because I didn't stay put in the house, available whenever her teenage kids cared to drop in.

"It's too late now," I continued, "and besides, it won't be more than twenty minutes by car." Mie rested a hand on my arm. "Ellinor, I think Stefan is feeling that you're dissociating." I withdrew my arm under the pretext of buttoning my cardigan. "I know very well that he's sore at me," I said. She paused. "Maybe *sore* isn't quite the right word," she continued. "There's a lot coming up when someone dies. Old feelings. I don't think he ever told you, but for many years, Stefan felt that their father was more interested in Morten. He's missed being seen and acknowledged by his dad. Of course that means a lot to a man. You were also more on a wavelength with Morten when they were young, because of his interest in art and so on. I don't mean to criticize you, but over the years, Stefan has been going about with this feeling, and now his father is suddenly gone."

She spoke softly, in a neutral tone of voice. Of course, we could discuss things openly, woman-to-woman, now that the men were so hopeless at all things emotional. "So that's why he was such a sourface," I said. She stared at me without blinking, as if I'd said something blasphemous. "I was wondering why he would sit like that, like he was injured or something," I continued. "Jesus Christ, Mie, how soft do you think he should be allowed to be? Your husband is forty-nine years old. He ought to have left that sort of thing behind ages ago. So he's missed being seen! He still wants to be praised? My goodness!" Mie blushed a little, but I couldn't gather if it was shame or anger. "I think you're being harsh," she said in the same subdued voice. "Harsh?" I repeated. "You know what, Mie? I think the two of you are being too sloppy. Too sloppy and self-centered, and way too domineering."

She looked as if I were some messenger from an alien planet, I tell you, Anna, but now the cap was off. I thought of Georg beneath all that soil, incapable of answering for himself. "It's no contradiction," I said. "Just look at Eliot and Franca. You crush them while you wrap them up in cotton wool. No one ever demanded anything from those kids; they don't even know how to handle a dishwashing brush, pampered as they are, always getting waited on by this or that Filipino maid." Mie's face had turned all white. "Joy is an au pair," she said. "I don't give a damn what you call your Negro," I answered, "but I worry about your children. I worry about how they're going to escape your embrace. How they will ever learn to think for themselves and be responsible people on their own. And you tell me that little Stefan, who is forty-nine, didn't feel that he was being seen . . ." Her eyes were full of contempt as she glided off the stool. "I don't think we're getting any further," she said and made for the entrance. "Thank you," I said in her direction. I didn't know why; the words just flew out of my mouth. I remained sitting and saw her cross the street and get into the dark-green four-wheel-drive and drive off without looking at me. You don't know how relieved I was. There is nothing like a conflict to do the difficult work for you. It is an underrated remedy, cowardly as we are, but it makes everything so much easier. Free at last, I thought, and stepped out to my bike.

I didn't go home. As I said, it is no longer my home, your house, our house; it is just a place like so many places. Home is somewhere else already, three empty rooms, so far, on a side street in Vesterbro. I checked that I had the key the real estate agent had given me and coasted to the station. The agent responded with astonishment when I turned to him, having looked around for less than a minute, and said that I wanted to buy. He murmured something about a house report. I asked when I could move in. He asked if I didn't want to think it over. "I never did," I said, "not when it was important."

The platform was empty, as if it had been the middle of the night. Only on the last bench did I see a tiny figure. I first thought that she was a child, the Filipino girl bending over her iPhone. Perhaps it was Joy, who also had a day off? As far as I know, they speak Spanish in the Philippines, but here the au pairs are called by English names, often slightly frivolous, much like the girls in a brothel. I am sorry, I lose myself; you have no idea what I'm talking about; but since you died, the women of the commercial upper middle classes have found a postcolonial solution to the difficult arithmetic problem of career multiplied with self-realization plus motherhood. You get yourself a third-world servant and call it cultural exchange, but nine out of ten live in the basement where the poor things can sit and Skype with the children they've had to leave behind with the grandparents in the palm hut.

I thought of Georg as I sat on the S-train and looked out on a wide stretch of parallel tracks, a welcome interruption of reddish-brown ballast and glistening rails among the self-sufficient greenery of the villa gardens. I never felt at home out here. You did, and you had no problem transplanting yourself from the bungalow at the end of Roskildevej that the emigrant worker from Salerno had been able to afford after years of moderation. You slipped into this fashionable environment just like that, and from day one you looked like Sophia Loren's little sister. I don't know if Georg felt at home, but I guess he might have settled in anywhere. He had that kind of calm. His self-reliance was so discreet that you couldn't tell it from his good-natured confidence in the world around him. I never knew anyone with a more undivided, whole-hearted goodwill, and I'm not saying this to give you a bad conscience or make you regret that you preferred to throw yourself into the arms of a more flighty,

dreamy man. Only later do we invent the reasons for
our love — I've learned that much. What was it that I
read somewhere? "Because it was him; because it was
me." It was even a man who wrote it, and it was just
about friendship.

But Georg. I remembered what Mie had said about
Stefan, and suddenly I got mad again. I became so
angry, so very angry, Anna, just recalling Georg's gentle,
heavy, ruddy features as the train passed the harbor. I
caught sight of a white ship, bright in the afternoon
sunlight, way out behind one of the fortress islands in
the sound. I concentrated on my remembrance of the
feeling in my fingertips when they followed the folds of
his thickset face, more slack after all those years, and I
promised myself that I would never, ever, go so low as
to defend him against his own children.

I got off at Vesterport and took the elevator from the
platform with my bike. The traffic was dense, and the
monotonous flow of sound and motion had a soothing
effect on me. The suburbs are so terribly quiet. I biked
through the theater passage and crossed Vesterbro Torv
in the direction of Istedgade. I couldn't help smiling.
Junkies, prostitutes, and Muslims — it wasn't a far cry.
Stefan would never understand. Your son has
out-grown me, Anna, and isn't that the way it should
be? I asked myself if Morten would be more inclined to
visit me on Amerikavej, but I didn't think so. He is a
leftist all right, but for him it's more of a cultural thing
than a question of solidarity with the lowly. You never

know what you'll be met with down there in terms of bad taste and unwholesome habits.

I continued until I reached my street. I've never been to America, and with my fear of flying I suppose I'll never go. Mind you, there are no boats crossing anymore, but I also don't know what I'd be doing there. The media are amply awash with images of America, and that will do. Georg never understood why I didn't feel like traveling. I'm afraid he missed a good deal because of me. I tried to explain to him that I felt alien enough where I was, even though I spoke the language, but I didn't develop the subject any further. I could sense from his look that I risked hurting him. If I was asked at dinner parties I would reciprocate by asking people what they thought they might get out of it. Sights are in any event more beautiful when photographed, and if you make do with pictures, you spare yourself the risk of bad weather and the trouble with finding a place where you can pee. Once you penetrate the exotic surface, everyday life in foreign lands has a disappointing resemblance to life at home. And if you stay on the surface for the sake of romance, you make yourself dumber than you need to be vis-à-vis the people you're romanticizing about. Besides, you only become melancholy from standing there as an outsider, spying on lives you'll never share.

Amerikavej. For years the name itself was all I needed in terms of travel. The street looks itself, and yet it doesn't. It's like taking two photographs on the same frame of film because you forgot to advance it, apart from the fact that no one uses film anymore. The lines double, the perspective seems to be slipping, and within that distance of smeared, skidding light I realize that most of my life is past me. I lingered for a few seconds at the front door, still with somebody else's name on it. Two empty rooms looking over the street and a third one, just as empty, facing the courtyard. The floorboards creaked and my steps resounded, giving me the feeling that I was intruding. Upon what? Emptiness itself, the absence of a stranger.

I wish that I could live here without any furniture or lamps. I would sit for days on end, leaning against a wall in the living room, and watch a beam of sunlight as it passed along the opposite wall, across the ceiling, out of sight. Watch the fading day and how darkness would rise forth from the bottom of the street. Listen to the traffic's distant mumbling, voices on the sidewalk, an ambulance, a radio playing somewhere. It was like sitting in a parenthesis, a bubble beyond it all, as it carried on without me. I looked at the outlines on the wall, slightly paler, where the previous residents had their furniture or pictures. It had never occurred to Georg that I might one day be sitting in a place like this or come to live here. I told myself that the thought of it would hurt me when I moved in, but it would have hurt even more had I remained in a place of which he knew every inch. You must pick the more suitable pain, and I was never one to look back.

It is so unfamiliar. I also never brooded over death or my getting older. Why would I want to do that? What else would I become? Did you consider death? Did you know that this might be — no, had to be — the end?

43

Did you have time to think so? I've always said to myself that I'll just proceed for as long as I can. I've said to myself that I should be happy as long as I'm able to move, as long as it doesn't hurt particularly much anywhere. I was never very deep, although you insisted on the reverse. I can talk and talk once I get started, but you were the profound one, in tune with, well, I wouldn't even know with what. With something I was never even close to understanding. When did you know that things were going wrong? You must have lost him in the snow. There must have been a moment, a few long seconds, when you were completely alone, but still conscious, in the middle of the whiteness.

We were so happy, do you remember? It was an impromptu party in the sleeper car, cheese and ham and a bottle of Chianti wrapped in raffia. We were still young; it was still adventurous to take a train going south. You had called your parents from a pay phone at the central station in Hamburg to say good night to the twins. When you joined us on the platform it was as if you'd let go of the last mooring; you were exuberant, full of crazy whims. He was your lover already, and nothing in the world would have seemed more remote to me. We belonged together, the four of us, all the way through Germany. We changed trains in Munich and continued to Bolzano, where we changed again. You knew a resort in the Dolomites, and you'd called to book rooms for us. I had never been as far away before. I had never been farther than the Baltic Sea.

Once we entered our room, I opened the window. It was late winter, and the snow on the summits resembled torn lace where the gray-blue mountainside showed through. I remained standing for a long time. There was a squeaking under people's boots as they passed below me along the tall snowdrifts. Henning came up to me and put his long arms around my waist. I remember that moment very clearly. The strange penumbra of the valley after the sun had passed below the ridge across from us. The rawness of the cold in my nostrils. His arms and chest behind me, which I could lean into as if we would never be anything but together. You must allow me to place that image here, Anna. We must look at it together; please don't lower your eyes. The worst thing was to lose you, but the second worst thing was that you never got a chance to ask for my forgiveness. You don't hear what I am saying, and that is the worst. You don't remember; you are not. I speak to you only because I want to be something more than an accumulation of facts and their succession.

Henning was good at skiing and you were also pretty sharp, while Georg had done mostly cross-country in Norway. After I'd spent a few mornings with a ski instructor, Georg offered to take me onto one of the easy tracks. It became our daily routine: The two of you took to the heights while Georg and I went skiing among families with children. I clung to him in the lift and didn't dare to look down. In the late afternoon we had drinks at the hotel's fireplace. You spoke all at once about the view from up there, and Georg listened, smiling in a good-natured way. I think he would have liked to join you and try himself in the terrain. I remember urging him to go with you, but he just smiled. Neither you nor Henning said anything that morning about going farther up than the previous days. The announcement came shortly past noon, and you still hadn't returned. Several avalanches were reported in the area; no one could say how many. Others were missing, too, but they showed up little by little. The authorities finally dared to begin the search a couple of hours before darkness fell.

Henning was never found. You were flown directly to a hospital in Bolzano, and we didn't get to see you until midnight. You were in a coma. They told us that you had been unconscious when you were found under the snow. Georg and I took turns sitting next to your bed through the night. In the morning, we spoke to a doctor who told us that lack of oxygen had probably caused serious brain damage. Georg went out to find a hotel. I stayed next to you, looking at your beautiful, immovable face. When he came back a few hours later, he had been to the ski resort to pick up our things. He had packed your suitcase and Henning's and mine. He had been standing in our room among all our stuff. I could see him in my mind, embarrassed at Henning's toothbrush. We didn't know what to say to each other when we had dinner in a restaurant near the hospital.

We stayed on in Bolzano. Georg had to call his office and ask for a few days off. They kept looking for Henning, but after a couple of days they stopped the search. Later on, I saw a paragraph from *Berlingske Tidende*, which had appeared on a page before the classified ads. *Dane disappears in the Alps*. It felt as if it had nothing to do with Henning. You were also mentioned, *a young Danish woman of Italian descent*, as if there were some connection between the accident and your father. Georg called him on the first night in Bolzano. He asked his parents-in-law not to say anything to the twins.

Neither one of us knew how to express our feelings. Grief doesn't always bring people together, as they say. Whatever we felt was blocked at the thought of the feelings of the other, and we said the most stupid, unimportant things, just to endure each other's company. I spent the days at your bedside. You lay like some Sleeping Beauty. Georg would sit there, too, but he couldn't take it for very long, your immobility in the respirator, as if you were already dead. Your calm breathing, as if you would open your eyes in a few seconds and recognize us and smile. Your conspiratorial, intelligent smile, was it to be erased forever from your face, whether you woke or slept on? I thought of the years we'd known each other, all the hours we'd spent together. I had trusted that they were being kept within both of us like linen in a drawer, ironed and folded, one set of them for each of us. It dawned on me only now how I'd believed that memory could be something to be had in common. I had seen you become a mother, grow into that role, extract that sort of authority from the girl you still were. You had seen me let go of my fear, ever so slowly, my fear of being found out.

I called my mother after they'd given up on finding Henning. I couldn't remember when I'd ever heard her cry, and I didn't know how to comfort her. Henning's mother didn't cry when I called; she became silent, and I first thought that the connection had been disrupted. "So they don't know if he's dead," she finally said. "So they don't know it for sure?" I couldn't think of a way to answer her. We had been in Bolzano for most of a week when Georg and I sat in the hotel bar late in the evening. Neither of us felt like going up to lie in the darkness, fully awake. I sensed that he had been drinking more than he used to. He'd had a conversation with the doctors earlier in the day. They had almost decided to declare that you were brain-dead, and they had prepared him for the only right decision, which would be to turn off the respirator. He sat for a long time looking into the bottles behind the bar, lined up in front of a mirror. It seemed as if he'd forgotten that I was sitting next to him.

"I saw them," he finally said. He was snuffling and spoke in such a hushed voice that I had to bend forward to distinguish his words from the music in the background. All of a sudden he turned to me, and I withdrew instinctively. "In our room," he said and stared fixedly. There was something surprisingly hard, almost evil, about his drunken eyes. It had happened on our second day at the resort. He had forgotten his scarf and returned to fetch it. You and Henning stood in front of the window. You had just time to let go of him as Georg entered, but only just. Throughout the years I have imagined the scene as if I'd been present myself, you and Henning at the window, both of you silent, Georg in front of the drawer or an open suitcase, silent, too, until he found his scarf and walked out without

48

turning around. Did any of you speak when he had gone? Did you embrace again? Had Georg left you in a silence so heavy that it was still oppressing you, forcing you through the doorway and into the elevator without a word, like guilty children?

I didn't notice a thing; the day resembled the previous one and those that followed until you were caught in an avalanche. Only in the evening did you and Georg get to be alone together, when we'd had our drinks at the fireplace and eaten and had fun. I really think we were having fun like we used to, but I have a blind angle here. He told me that he hadn't said anything when you returned to your room. He wanted to wait and allow you to begin. You said that nothing had happened. He didn't answer, and his silence became a trap when you responded by falling silent yourself, withdrawn and sulky. Your mutual silence prevented him from asking or confronting you with the little signs that confirmed for him in retrospect that he'd seen what he'd seen. Little breaches in your everyday pattern. One evening you hadn't been there when he came home from the office. You hadn't shown up until an hour and a half later, strangely distracted while the boys kept asking where you'd been. One morning shortly after, Henning had called, and he hadn't been able to conceal his surprise when Georg answered the phone. But did he really try to conceal it?

The next day you and Georg were waiting for us in front of the hotel. I still see you with your skis, alone together, exposed to the mountains and each other. Georg told me that he'd asked you straightaway. You

49

had looked at him, and your eyes had been unwavering as you answered him. Courageous Anna. He asked if you wanted a divorce. You said that you didn't know. Then we came up to you, and the four of us walked in the direction of the lifts, just like the day before.

Your father looked a stranger in the church, the immigrant from Salerno, a short, lean man in a suit that was too big for him. He seemed as insecure as he had been when the twins were baptized, still doubtful, after all those years, as to how things were done here. You weren't a Catholic; I sometimes forget that he had surrendered to his new country and allowed you to be raised a Protestant. You never took off the little gold cross that he'd given you for your confirmation, which had belonged to his mother. You wore it in your coffin. I don't recall what the priest said. I also remember nothing of the gathering afterward, although I'd helped Georg organize everything. I remember the hollow thud each time the priest let a shovelful of soil fall onto the coffin's lid. A tiny, narrow shovel like the ones the twins had played with in the sandbox.

I'd never heard that sound before. I was standing behind your parents and your parents-in-law, who had come over from Jutland. The boys were standing between Georg and your mother-in-law. I remember their slight necks in the March sun and their blond hair, cut short and ending in a tip on their napes. They've inherited Georg's colors; you would almost believe they were mine if it weren't for their brown eyes. To this day I am unaware how Georg got around

50

to telling them what had happened. You were just thirty, the boys were seven.

I came by often, helping him cook, or I fetched Stefan and Morten from school. I had nothing better to do after work, and it was a relief to help him out rather than sit at home, falling into myself. I knew my way around the house and where to find everything. After you moved we had been the ones to visit; you had plenty of space, and then there were the boys. Even so, it felt strange to let myself in with the key Georg had given to me. Luckily, the boys had always liked me. I would normally do the shopping on my way back from town so that I could fetch them and have the dinner ready when Georg came home. I was never the cook you were, but the twins were surprisingly polite, considering their age. One of the first times, I made tiramisu, but I shouldn't have done that. Usually, I said good night at the table. Georg had always been the one to read to them, and when he sat between them in the lower part of the bunk bed I felt how it would have been a violation by me, like infringing on a holy threshold, to bend over their boy faces, straighten their pillows, and kiss their cheeks. I heard them speak ever so reasonably with Georg about you watching them from a cloud.

I helped in clearing your closets and sorting out your stuff. There were no letters, not a trace. What did you have in mind? Time and again I've asked myself the same question. Would you have cleared your closets yourself one day and gathered your things? Divorces had become trendy, in the meantime, but you and I were never trendy. The world had gone electric and let its hair grow without us. You were still too Christian, after all, and I was still too much of I don't know what. Too cowed? Too doubtful of my own rightfulness? In the meantime, it had become trendy to screw whomever you wanted to screw, but you laughed once when I first used that word, making faces. One July afternoon in another age we were sprawling on a bathing jetty and talking about sex. How powerless the words had become, now that nothing was forbidden or just shameful any longer. *Fuck* remained too pornographic, but *screw*? You felt the same way about those words, and you laughed even louder when I asked what sex and work tools had to do with one another. What did you have in mind, Anna? I believe that you were honest that morning, standing in the snow, skis in your hands, bravely answering Georg's question. Don't know. Love doesn't know, does it? It only has its moment, for as long as it lasts.

As I walked about in your home, performing this or that basic function, I often considered what you might have thought of it. As I bent over to empty the washing machine, I sometimes felt as if you were watching me from between the closets in the semidarkness of the hallway. I didn't turn around, would not break the enchantment it was to imagine you standing out there, just a silhouette against the sunlight on the terrace. At times I would sit in the living room and close my eyes, and if one of the floorboards gave I would think, Here she comes. What would you have said to me? Would you have had an explanation? I don't think so, but since you never came, since the dead don't come, I had to explain for myself. I went much further by way of explaining than I think you'd ever have gone. Love produces its facts on the ground, like a bombshell at first, then like a long-term building project, and in due course the scandal and the rupture and the drama will no longer need explaining. There is what is. Love's bereaved ones are left to try and understand. It is for the rejected to be noble and wisely realize that we have each other only on loan. The lovers arrogate the right to themselves by force, or what resembles force, and they wouldn't dream of accounting for anything. Because it was him; because it was you. We who are no longer being loved must choose between revenge and understanding, and I thought that, yes, of course the two of you had to drift toward one another. I thought of the fanciful, the dark-haired and slightly adventurous quality about both of you. I would have preferred to be angry, had I been allowed to. I understood far too much, far too early.

When the boys were asleep, Georg and I would sit and talk for a while before I went home. He also wanted to understand. We talked about you as if you couldn't help it. Perhaps you couldn't, but as I biked up the avenue I felt completely scooped out with magnanimous, sorrowful understanding. I wondered if Georg felt that way, too, alone on the sofa in front of the TV set, and later on in the bed that had become too big for him. I let myself in, turned on the lights, and began to gather Henning's clothes and stuff, put it all into plastic sacks, and carried them into the basement where the garbage containers were. It would have been too scornful having to look at his shirts and shoes and his badminton racket as if he might return any minute.

Spring came, and we could eat outside in the evening if the weather was fine. When the white nights began, we might stay on with a glass of wine and more often we spoke of something else. He told me about himself, things I'd never known. He had grown up on a farm in Jutland, but he hadn't felt like working the land. Still, he missed the open country. He had once saved the neighbor's son from drowning in a marl pit. He had found a flint ax and taken it to school, and his history teacher had sent it to the national museum. He smiled in a bashful way, as if he didn't know himself why he told me things like that, stories without a point, bits and pieces of times past. To begin with, I feared that he would ask where I myself had grown up, but he didn't, content with sharing whatever happened to come to his mind. Usually, you had been the one to tell stories and let yourself go; Henning and you had taken turns expatiating while Georg and I listened. It all became so clear now, but I had never given it a thought. Only when you and I were alone together did I talk more freely. You said so once. You told me that I was like somebody else when we were on our own.

Georg, too, was like somebody else, or I felt that only now did I begin to know him, because he was allowed the room and the time to tell what he had seen when he was a boy and a young man. A private first class in the army, later on a sergeant. At first he had wanted to stay in the army, but then he ended up in insurance. He shrugged and smiled as if he himself wouldn't be able to say how this had happened. I listened, happy that he didn't ask any questions, happy to fantasize about a world I hadn't known, of furrows, barn wings, and seasons. He laughed when I opened my eyes wide because he knew both how to drive a tractor and how to take a machine gun apart and assemble it again. One evening in early summer we sat for a long time on the terrace. We had finished the better part of a bottle of wine when I got up in the twilight and made for my bike. He got up, too, his shirt brighter than his face, and I couldn't read him, only felt his eyes resting on me. He asked in a low voice if I didn't want to stay. I put a hand on his chest shortly and said no. He remained standing as I found my way out.

I could feel that I had been drinking when I followed the avenue through the pale evening. Everything seemed sharper, almost intrusive; there was a sighing in the tall poplars, and the glaring light from the streetlamps made me think of hyacinths. He must have looked at me that way for some time, but since when? Did it occur to him while we sat in the grainy dusk that would never give way to the night? Ellinor is a young woman. Ellinor has tanned knees already under the seam of her dress although it is only just June, her neck is long and downy, and her hands are slender and nice. Ellinor sleeps alone like I do. Perhaps he had opened his eyes to me while I brushed his boys' teeth or drained the boiled potatoes. Didn't I want to stay? What if I did? Life must go on, as they say. One can always ask.

I was unable to sleep. I lay awake and thought of Henning. I lay on the side of the bed that had always been mine. It was still an unfamiliar thing, not to have his back and shoulder as a barrier between myself and the French window where the folds of the curtain moved in the chink of cool night air. His back had been a firmament of birthmarks. He couldn't sleep in anything but shorts, even in winter. Did you ever get to spend a whole night together? I couldn't begin to understand how you'd gotten the opportunity to fuck or screw, or whatever, in such a way that I never suspected anything. When did the right conditions occur? I suppose you needed to wash afterward. It does require certain measures: a bed somewhere, an hour under the marital radar. Did you check into a hotel? Perhaps I am being too conformist. Am I to think in terms of beaches and forests? But when, Anna? And what about the overtures, shifting gears from being friends to something more? I have such a hard time imagining this — what you say, how you do it. Did it happen while you were dancing? We always danced at parties; it is one of the few times when you're allowed to touch without being a couple.

You were a marvelous dancer. So was Georg; he really knew how to swing a woman around, but strangely enough the safety of his movements made it wholly unerotic. The dance became a scheme, a convention, not the prelude to something else. On the other hand, I never tired of watching the two of you dance together. Henning may have become aware of you that way, while you were dancing with Georg.

That's a couple, if ever there was one; we all thought the same: she belongs to him, he only has eyes for her, and their dancing is the cooled lineament of their passion. One could only be envious. There is a picture that was taken at a dance contest several years before we met you. The photographer has caught Georg just as he turns his face to look you in the eyes. You are dancing a slowfox, each of you with a number on your back; you are wearing a balloon skirt; you love him.

Georg found the photograph in a shoe box when I helped him go through your remaining things. A box full of images from your life. We had sorted out your clothes and given them to the Salvation Army. There were also snapshots of Henning and myself together with one of you, depending on who had taken the picture. None of them included the four of us. We squatted in the hallway with closet doors made of teak. You never liked those closets, but they were there when you bought the house, and space always comes in handy. I can still hear you pronouncing the remark in a matter-of-fact tone. It was a Saturday in early summer; your father had fetched the twins and taken them to a soccer tournament. A ray of sunlight penetrated into the narrow hallway and fell over the black-and-white photo from a dance contest in the beginning of the 1960s. The distant past already, I thought, and propped up the picture on my knees, suddenly conscious that Georg was looking at me. "She is beautiful," I said, determined not to look into his eyes. I had behaved as if nothing had happened after the evening on the terrace when he'd asked if I wanted to stay. What else would I do? He had seemed relieved, I thought, almost grateful that I'd let his words pass as if they'd never been spoken.

I wanted to get up, but I was afraid of becoming dizzy. I tend to be dizzy if I get up too suddenly, and I stayed put in the same awkward position, squatting with my knees tight, caught by his gaze as I sank the corners of the photograph into the skin of my kneecaps. The boys weren't there, so we had the house to ourselves — he must have thought something like that. The conditions were right. I told him that I was going to see my mother. It was true, but my words sounded like an admission that I'd read his mind. "Yes," he said and was the first to get up. I stayed for a second with the old pictures because I didn't want to rush out of the house.

The slanting beam of sunlight had receded into the corner next to the last window, as if it had pulled backward through the dust on the windowpanes. I looked around the empty apartment, as much of it as I could see from where I was sitting, leaning against the wall. This was a place where I wouldn't for even a fleeting moment imagine that Georg might come through the door and call my name. Here I couldn't even imagine the sound of his steps, the sound of the floorboards under him as he crossed the room. It came over me once more, like an attack, the pressure from within. The feeling that I was being driven out of myself by a claustrophobic, growing mass that made me swell. For a few desperate seconds, I could not breathe. Then

I began to cry and fell over along the panel, crouching until it was over.

I let the hour pass, although the floor was hard to sit on. Each noise I made rang through the empty apartment. Half an hour later, the low sunrays flushed with the indentations of the dirty brownstone facade on the other side of the street. A golden echo, like a double exposure. I got up and closed my eyes until the faint bout of dizziness had gone off. I opened a window and sat on the windowsill, looking into the street. There had been fewer cars parked along the curb back then, but the light of a late afternoon remained the same. For an instant, I expected to hear children's voices resound between the walls, a flock of them, spreading and coming together like sparrows.

I was neither the oldest nor the youngest, just one of the pack, racing in and out of gateways, through the backyards and cellarways, around the corner to the butcher's if someone had a few coins to spend on cracklings. This was a raw, snotty, unswerving brother- and sisterhood, kept together by the fear of perverts, the fear of punishment, the unreasonable enthusiasm for simple things. Raw, snotty pleasures, a rat cornered by the older boys, a penny found on the sidewalk and realized on the spot for toffees or Finnish licorice. The grown-ups had no idea of our whereabouts. Most of the time, most of them didn't care much, either, and our expeditions would take us as far as the park around Frederiksberg Castle or the harbor's southern end where we played among the heaps of coal. Invariably, I came home with my clothes torn, and my mother always worried about me, but in her case it was an attitude rather than a notion of real threats, apart from the perpetual stories about flashers and indecency.

My thin, frightened little mother. She laundered and mangled for people and worked as a cleaning woman in a school, not mine, thank God, and she could just make ends meet, bursting from the effort. She had been beautiful, almost as beautiful as you were, and the proof had been framed in gold, with a flap on the back, and placed between a porcelain nymph and a leather-bound edition of the *Dictionary of the Danish Language* that I'd never seen her open. I opened it myself when it was raining and I couldn't go out. I read the words, column after column, as I waited for the rain to stop. My mother had been a buxom beauty from Stege, but the years and the hardships had made every part of her shrink except for the nose, which made her look like a clipped puffin, immovable on its cornice in the storm.

I bent forward in the open window and caught a glimpse, farther down the street, of our front door. A tricycle, rickshaw-style, was parked in front, and next to it a young Pakistani fellow stood smoking in trousers several sizes too big. He turned around as another fellow came out. They made a high five and continued along the sidewalk, shoulders stooping and their feet turned outward. My mother didn't get to see the neighborhood change. She wasn't even sixty when she died; for more than ten years I have been older than her, and I still haven't gotten used to it. My mother, a younger woman.

60

As usual, she first opened the door a crack until she recognized me and then closed it to take off the chain. I entered the living room before her and pushed the spinning wheel standing in a corner in memory of a rustic past even she had never known. "Why don't you get rid of this hulk," I said and watched the spokes of the wheel turn more slowly and finally come to a halt. I always asked when I came to see her, and she always remained silent, offended in a dignified way. She had put cups on the table, the ones with blue flowers on them. I handed her a paper bag of pastries, and as she stood in the kitchen, arranging them on a dish, I looked at the picture from her confirmation, resplendent with the defenseless trust of her youth. She sat on the sofa, and I got to sit in the armchair. "Still no news?" She put a finger on the lid of the china pot as she poured coffee into my cup. "They won't find him," I said. "It's difficult to believe," she said. "You know how much I loved him. And Anna, of course," she added. "They were having an affair," I said. I hadn't even decided to tell her; I just said it. At first she looked as if she hadn't understood. "Don't say a thing like that," she said. "It's the truth," I said.

She put a lump of sugar into her cup and stirred mechanically while lifting the saucer. It would have been more affectionate of me to keep it to myself. I realized that I was burdening her with my own homeless anger. "How's her husband doing, all alone with those boys?" She put her cup and saucer on the table and folded her hands in her lap as she looked at me. "He's fine," I said. "He's quite practical, you know." "You might help him out now and then," she said. "Yes, I might," I said. "I am sure he'd appreciate that," she said. I shrugged. We became silent, as usual. One could hear the clock again, sluggishly marking time with its dreary weights between yellowed walls. I cast a sidelong glance at the framed picture of a young, trusting girl. It was the only thing she'd brought with her when she left her hometown one evening, sheltered by the darkness, with a baby girl in her arms. "It seems as if history repeats itself," she said. "What do you mean?" I asked. She looked at me for a while before she continued, and the perpetual fearfulness in her eyes gave way to sadness and calm. "Now your husband has also disappeared. Just like your father," she said in a low voice. "My father didn't disappear," I said. "The war was not an avalanche; the war was the war. I suppose he walks about somewhere, for all we know." She looked down at her hands. "The war was an avalanche," she said.

I was surprised at myself when I sat on the bus. I could have told her about my afternoons with Georg and the boys. Had it been the thought of her recognition that I could not bear? I spotted a girl at a crosswalk, holding on to a woman with one hand and a large, striped lollipop with the other. She'd probably been to the Tivoli Gardens. I remembered that I'd promised Stefan and Morten a bag of Saturday goodies each, and I bought two bags of licorice allsorts at the station kiosk. Sitting on the S-train on my way out of town, I saw the picture again of a younger Georg with a firm hold on your waist as you're dancing a slowfox, looking each other in the eyes. I continued one stop more than usual before I got off and hurriedly crossed the viaduct. I didn't quite know the way and had to follow my instinct. A tournament like that probably lasted most of the day, but it was getting late.

After a few minutes, I could follow the distant sound of boys' voices, drowned from time to time by a strident whistle. I followed the wire fence along the grounds, looking for an entrance and watching the boys in multi-colored shirts as they ran on the grass or stood with the grown-ups and followed the game. I was afraid that I wouldn't recognize Stefan and Morten, or catch sight of your father. I hadn't expected Georg to have joined them, but maybe that had been the agreement from the outset. He hadn't seen me yet. I stopped a few steps from the cluster of parents anxiously following the match. The cheers became louder; apparently someone was about to score. He smiled, clenched his right fist, and put his left arm around your father's shoulders. I stood still until he turned his head and saw me.

I took the place you left behind. I took over your life, Anna, as I'd once taken over your wedding dress. It wasn't as difficult as one might have thought. The boys started on the sweets once they were in the backseat, dirt and grass all over their shorts and socks. Georg looked at me out of the corner of his eyes while he was driving. Your father followed in his own car. He had made lasagna at home; the roasting pan was in his trunk. Morten asked if I would stay for dinner, and Georg looked at me again. For the first time I felt like a visitor, but I would stay until the boys had been put to bed and your father had left. We stepped out onto the terrace with our glasses. I asked him if he would teach me how to dance a slowfox. He looked at me for a while before he smiled. That way, I thought, we might allow ourselves to touch, even if we weren't a couple. "Now?" he asked. I nodded and rose from my chair.

While we were eating lasagna, your father turned to me and asked if I remembered the time when you brought me to his and your mother's place out on Roskildevej. He had also made lasagna then. It must have been ten years ago. It was the only time I'd visited your childhood home, but he talked of it as if only a few months had passed. He spoke about my visit as if it were something important. I'd never thought of it that way; I'd almost forgotten about it. You never came home with me on Amerikavej, and we didn't even talk about it. I also don't think that you felt as if you had given yourself away, like I would. I have a clear memory of the little bungalow, the tiny front garden, the narrow concrete walkway behind the wrought-iron fence. One hundred and twenty-five square meters, that must have been it, but enough to make a world as long as you're a child. I envied your affection as you put your arms around your father, who was a head shorter than you, and your tubby mother, who laughed at his pronunciation and corrected him all the time. It stung in a secret place to see the three of you together, because I came to think of my mother and how awkward we could be.

64

Your mother laughed away because your father was the one who did the cooking, but she was proud, nevertheless, I could feel that. Everything was so meticulous in your living room, the tablecloth and the embroidered napkins, and your father had opened a bottle of wine. He told you off when you took it and wanted to fill the glasses. He had taught you a hundred times not to hold the bottle with your hand turned away from the person you were pouring out for; that was an insult. I almost got frightened by his tone, but you just laughed; apparently it wasn't as bad as one might think from listening to him. "*Pour*," your mother said, "not *poor*," and then he also laughed. There was a picture on the wall, an oil painting of the slick sort, a rocky island rising from the blue, blue sea. I asked him if he was from Capri. "Salerno," he said and dried his mouth with the back of his hand. You explained to me where Salerno was, and I asked how he'd ended up in Denmark. You and your mother watched him attentively as if you'd never heard the story before. How you'd become possible.

I remembered it again as he sat across from me, between Georg and his grandchildren, a thin, furrowed man with hollow temples, salt and pepper in his close-cropped hair. I tried to guess what he might have looked like before the war, the young sailor from Salerno who had signed off in Copenhagen. You intervened in his account; it hadn't been Copenhagen only, you said, and you told me how he'd met a fellow his age, in a bar in Nyhavn, and heard of the cryolite adventure in Greenland. They worked up there the whole summer, he added, and spent the winter in Copenhagen living on the money they'd earned. He grinned, exposing his gold teeth; they'd lived like kings, but then the war came, and he was stranded. He got a job in a factory making tools for the Germans. One had to make a living, he said with a shrug, and that was where he'd had his training. After the Liberation he had planned to go home, but Salerno was just about flattened, people lived like dogs, and then he ran into your mother.

And my own father, what about him? I suppose that he wanted to be polite, in order that the conversation shouldn't focus on the host only, but he could see from your expression that he'd put his foot in it. You didn't know anything, but you must have felt that I disliked being asked. "I've never known my father," I said and smiled. "The war," I added and gestured vaguely. "The war," your father said again and looked down at his plate before he turned to you and asked you to pour us some more wine. "And don't stick your elbow in our noses when you hold the bottle," he continued on a light note. "*Hold*, not *whole*," your mother said. I avoided looking at you, relieved when she asked me about my job in the advertisement department.

The war was the war. The war had been an avalanche. Some had disappeared, and others had just come to live a different life than they had expected, in a different world. I would have liked to talk to you about my father. You are the only one I would have liked to tell who he was, except that I hardly know myself. Why was it that I could never summon up the courage to do it? I never told Henning anything, nor Georg. They must have thought, both of them, that I had never known him. Since my mother died, nobody knows who I am. Both Henning and Georg must have sensed that they weren't supposed to ask me. Perhaps they assumed that he must be dead, but that Sunday, when you and I went to see your parents, he would probably have been alive. He was still only in his fifties, and in all likelihood he lived an ordinary life in some part of Germany. We didn't even have a picture of him; we had only his name, Thomas Hoffmann. Quite common as a name. I never even thought to look for him, never.

I know that it's too late to tell you about it, but it isn't pointless. If other people knew that I am sitting here writing to you, they would worry about me. Stefan wouldn't want to hear about it, and Mie would send me to a psychologist — she has a solution to everything. None of them would be capable of comprehending that it may be hopeless and completely meaningful at the same time. It is in the words that they must be addressed to someone. If not, they just line up in the dictionary, waiting for the rain to stop. You're allowed to take them into your possession but only if you pass them on in the same breath. You can't just sit and hold them back; that way they come to naught. I wouldn't be telling the story if it wasn't for you, if it wasn't for me. But it is you, it always was, and I would like to tell you about my parents. I would like to tell you about Sigrid and Thomas.

★   ★   ★

She wasn't even twenty. Her father had been employed in a gravel pit nearby, but he got bad lungs and had to stop. He could do nothing but sit at home, wheezing; the sound permeated the apartment, it even reached her through the wall to her small room. My grandmother was a matron at the hotel; that was how she got Sigrid a job in the taproom. Sigrid waited on the guests in the evening, and during the day she served in a bakery. As I said, she was pretty, and she didn't mind getting things done. The baker would like to see her engaged to his son, but she wasn't interested. She read in her bed before she went to sleep. Her mother told her to be careful that she didn't end up needing glasses. That would be a shame, she said, as pretty as she was. But Sigrid kept on reading, and she told herself that life could be something more than this. She didn't know exactly what, and she didn't need to; in fact, it was better that way, not knowing. She did not want to know what the future held, but she knew that it would present itself somewhere other than Stege. Her future would never call on her in a place like this, she might have said that to anyone who asked her, and she prepared for the day when she would have to break out and go to meet it.

The German officers liked to frequent the hotel. Every night they sat at a corner table in the taproom; eventually they were the only ones left apart from the contractors and businessmen who traded with the Wehrmacht. The other men in town stayed away, much to the disquiet of the proprietor, my mother told me. At this time, everyone knew which way things were going, except for the collaborationists in the taproom and the regulars at the German table. People talked hushedly among themselves about the war and how it would probably last for another year, at the most, but at the officers' table they only became louder and more cheerful as the months went by. Manners were like that at their table, and new faces were quick to adapt. When the seas ran high they would start singing until the proprietor reminded them politely that it was after hours. Of course, Sigrid had to stay until the guests were gone and the dishes done. It would often be way past midnight before she could go to sleep. The officers were pretty taken by her, in all friendliness most of the time, and she was nice about it; she just smiled and let it bounce off her. She could feel that the proprietor was pleased to see how popular she was and how she handled it. Sometimes he gave her something special to take back home, a rolled-meat sausage, a pound of coffee, and other treasures. The officers would also tip her at times, and she accepted, with some reluctance. She would certainly hesitate when they were drunk and gave her to understand, smiling and winking, how sweet they thought she was.

One late evening in August, they were even more vociferous than usual. The taproom was empty except for the usual crowd of officers around the regular table. They blurred in their uniforms, and she hadn't yet noticed the latest face. It was a warm evening and it didn't help that the windows couldn't be opened due to the blackout curtains. Several officers had opened their jackets, and they were drinking heavily. One of them had lit a cigar, and as she served another round of beers he suddenly grasped her around the waist and forced her down on his lap. She expected him to let go of her straightaway when she felt his hand around one of her breasts and pulled away with such force that he fell backward with his chair. There was a roar of laughter while she stood completely paralyzed and watched the presumptuous, flushing officer pick himself up. She had just the time to notice the only one of them who didn't laugh. She hadn't seen him before, younger than the others and still with his uniform jacket correctly buttoned, pale and motionless. The proprietor came running, alerted by the turmoil, and she raced past him into the kitchen. She could hear the party leaving and the proprietor good-humoredly accepting their apologies in broken German. He allowed her to go home before the place was cleared, but she remained standing for several minutes in the darkness behind the kitchen entry until it was completely silent outside.

The air was almost as warm as it had been in the taproom, and the laden harvest moon was low over the cove. She wheeled her bike across the courtyard and was about to mount it when the gravel crunched behind her back and made her start. The young officer stepped out of a shadow and took off his cap in a ceremonious way that would have made her smile if he hadn't frightened her. She had been good at German in school, and she almost understood everything he said. He wanted to apologize. She said that he'd done nothing wrong. He said that he felt ashamed of having been sitting at the same table. They walked together;

there was no one else in the street, but in the silence it felt as if everybody must be hearing each word. He'd been transferred recently and didn't know the town. She said that he would have to be careful not to lose his way. There was something ever so courteous about his manner that incited her to tease him a bit. She could hear from his voice that he smiled. Perhaps it was best if he didn't accompany her much longer? Yes, perhaps, she said.

That's how my mother's love story began. She thought of him when she'd returned to her small room, and the next day, until she thought of him no longer. She didn't see anything of him the following days; he was not at the regular table in the evening, nor the evening after. The others were more quiet than usual, and the cigar smoker who had groped her breast made a point of being distinguished and aloof. She'd almost forgotten the short conversation in the August night when suddenly one afternoon, the polite young officer stood in the bakery where she served. He looked as if he, too, was taken by surprise. There were other customers in the shop, and when it became his turn he just looked fixedly at her for a second before he asked for a cake. He has a sweet tooth, she thought, and she suppressed a smile. He paid and left, and she served the next customer, glad that he hadn't revealed that they'd met before. But what would he have had to say? She became irritated with herself for thinking about him. He was more handsome in daylight than she remembered him. A narrow face, green eyes, sandy hair, it seemed.

"You look like him," my mother said. She told me the story on New Year's Eve when I was fourteen. We were always on our own during Christmas and the New Year; she had only me. She'd lived that way ever since we came to Copenhagen — secluded, on the alert. Until then, I'd thought that my father had died when I was a baby. I asked if she'd never considered the fact that he was German. "To begin with, yes," she answered.

A few evenings later he was at the regular table again. He avoided looking at her when she served, and he left before the others. When she was free, he stood waiting in the courtyard. He accompanied her some of the way, like the first evening. It happened several times; he would wait, and they walked next to each other, through the streets to begin with, or in the direction of the cove. She never told me when he kissed her for the first time, and of course she was too shy to tell me how they found a place where they could be together. She kept that to herself, and I haven't even tried to imagine it. You will have to what without the details, Anna, like I have. All I know is that they were as careful as you can be in a small town. She never walked down the street on his arm as did the other German-loving sluts, intoxicated by their own conceit, or just stupid. She looked at me. "You're the daughter of a German loving slut," she said with an eerie smile. "Now you know."

The single risk he allowed himself was to come into the bakery every afternoon, buy a cake, and keep a straight face as he met her eyes. It was only reluctantly that he'd begun to show up in the taproom again. He was afraid it might cause suspicion among the others if he stayed away and one of them thought to combine his absence with the cigar-smoking officer's assault. He was touchingly cautious, almost timid. It wasn't exactly what you might have expected from a soldier. They met at night out at the cove, on the overgrown paths along the meadows. They could talk ever so freely, as if they'd known each other for a long time. He was from a village close to Weimar, where his father owned a small printing house. He spoke of Goethe and recited to her. He wanted to know which books she cared for, and he couldn't comprehend that she'd never read Ibsen. His dream was to become a stage director. When it happened he would stage *The Lady from the Sea*. He retold the story about the woman in the fjord who is waiting for a sailor. He has said to her that he will come back one day and take her with him. In spite of that she marries someone else, a widower with grown-up daughters; and you know what, Anna? The sailor *comes* at last. When she asks her husband to release her, and he brings himself to do so, she decides to stay with him at the very last moment. "Later on, I thought that it seemed as if Thomas had tried to make me understand something," my mother said. It was curious to hear her mention him by his first name, but it was actually even more curious that I should be surprised. A young German called Thomas, still not my father. "But I didn't marry," she said. "And he didn't come," she added after a pause.

One evening in the autumn they were following the track between the meadows and the reeds. The last formations of migrant birds had already passed over the Baltic Sea. She and Thomas had been watching them one Sunday. Each of them had defied all security measures, as if driven by the same impulse, and taken to their customary meeting place in the clear October sun. They had seen it as proof of their intimacy, two minds with but a single thought, yet in the wind and the darkness he was gloomy. The war would end soon, he said. In a few months' time Hitler would have lost everything, and her country, all of Europe, would be liberated. Later, she wondered how he could have seen everything so clearly. He pulled her close, told her he would come back one day, "*in einem anderem Anzug.*"

You can't help imagining the two of them together, can you? In front of the windswept, brackish water behind the rush. She is standing by her black lady's bicycle as he hugs her, lean and angular in his uniform. At some point, she has given herself to him. I know it sounds old-fashioned, Anna, but I can't use any of the other words available. They didn't screw, they didn't fuck, not that way, and it is not that I want to make them more pure than they were. Only I'm certain it was something other than lechery that made the difference. It's not that I wish to romanticize unduly, but who says that the truth must always be crude? Stefan thinks so when he's had a bit too much of his California red wine while he grills steaks on the terrace. When Mie has to calm him down with an admonitory hand on his nape, not because he's being uncivilized but because it's uncool to reduce all human striving to tits and pricks.

74

It's not that I want to romanticize. What is a love story? Two young people who feel driven toward each other. She was nineteen, he was going on thirty while they were together. She gave him a silver spoon, her most precious possession. It had been given to her as a christening gift, and apart from everything else, she had to bear her mother's silent disappointment that she'd allowed the spoon to become lost. Somewhere in Germany, there is a silver spoon with her name engraved in italics on the handle. Perhaps his children inherited it. Perhaps they let it pass on, with a shrug, to the secondhand dealer who collected the things they couldn't use. Or some great-grandchild eats yogurt with it, and they remain ignorant, all of them, of where it started its journey toward that chubby little German hand, far or not so far from Weimar. My mother didn't even remember the name of the village where his father had a printing house — which had probably been bombed to rubble anyway, like so much else. There was no way of knowing his whereabouts in that devastated country where shabby, anonymous bands drifted around, and where it was impossible to distinguish the ruins of one city from the ruins of another. She wouldn't have had the slightest idea where to start looking for some Thomas Hoffmann, a former officer in the German occupying troops in Denmark, that is, if she'd decided to try.

As the years went by, anyone else would have brushed it aside as a youthful infatuation, in this case an aberration, since we all know how the hormones are simmering at that age. How you can get butterflies in your stomach if only someone's gaze rests upon you a little while longer than expected. There's no reason to exaggerate; or, to put it differently, you would search in vain for a deeper reason except that it was her, and that it was him. It could have been a different young man, no doubt about it, but it wasn't. The facts of a life become so enigmatic when that life is over. There is just that silver spoon somewhere, the rest is guessing, but the coincidence of it all is no reason to slander the defenseless trust of youth. Yes, they were inexperienced; they had but Goethe and Ibsen and whatever world literature she'd been devouring in her bed, but why should hormones and coincidence be weightier? Don't we make ourselves poorer, with all our knowledge, than we need to be, only because we can?

You couldn't see that she was pregnant when Denmark was liberated. So far she only suspected it herself. In the tense atmosphere permeating the small town, she and Thomas hadn't seen each other for several weeks. Every night she waited at the kitchen entrance of the hotel before she got on her bike. She had been out at the cove a couple of times before she went home. The regular table was empty, and on the night when the message of liberation was broadcast, new customers poured into the taproom. She was in a torpor as she served the liberated while the streets resounded with excitement. She recognized the baker's son among the jubilant, drunken faces. He clasped her cheek in a frisky way. "Look happy!" he shouted at her, and she smiled the best she'd learned and hurried on with her tray full of beer bottles. There had been a touch of something in his eyes. When she returned to the counter, the proprietor handed her an envelope, staring at her fixedly. She stuck it under her apron without looking at it and rushed to open a new relay of bottles. Someone had ripped the blackout curtains from the windows and opened them wide, and the noise inside mingled with the exhilarated voices in the street.

She didn't read his letter until she came home late at night. Had he been to deliver it himself? As she sat in her small room it felt as if the proprietor's expressionless gaze were still resting upon her. The first thing that struck her was that she hadn't known his handwriting. So much about him remained unknown to her, and in her thoughts she clung to each of the few words he'd scribbled with tiny, cramped letters. He wrote that he expected to be deported within a very short time. He wrote that he would come back again, that he would not forget her.

Shortly after, she stood in the crowd watching the German soldiers march past on their way out of town. There was no doubt any longer — she was long overdue. She tried in vain to catch a glimpse of him among the empty faces. She stood on tiptoe, stretching her neck, when all of a sudden someone grasped her arm firmly so that she almost fell. At first she didn't recognize the baker's son in the flat steel helmet. He was also wearing the armband of the resistance, but she couldn't imagine his having performed in any important way with his pale, doughy hands. She was taken to the school and pushed into the gymnasium.

She recognized the smell of sweat and floor polish between the lacquered wall bars and floorboards, lusterless from the footprints. She also recognized some of the faces on the line, regulars from the taproom, several of them belonging to the most enterprising people in town. There were other girls, and they all avoided looking at each other. The proceedings were of a shrill, bedraggled kind. She was questioned about the letter, and in her mind's eye she saw once more the proprietor and his unfathomable gaze. She supposed nothing else would have paid him, now that his clientele had been replaced so abruptly. They had been seen together after all, by whom or where, she could not conceive. She and the other girls had their hair cut off before they were taken through town on an open truck. As she lowered her eyes, listening to the jeering crowd, she asked herself if she would have been treated the same had it been visible that she was expecting.

Her father never spoke to her again. She only heard him wheeze at night, through the wall, when she lay awake. Her mother said hardly anything, either. I have never known them; I don't even have a picture of them. That summer, Sigrid stayed in the house. It was the loveliest weather, and everybody was so happy. She sat in the living room when her mother had gone to work and her father took a nap, or she stayed in her room. During the first weeks she hoped that there would be a letter from Germany, but he didn't even have her address. Was any mail at all coming out of that bombed-out country? In the night, she sneaked out of the house and biked to the path along the cove, unaccustomed to the sensation of cool air on her scalp and nape.

She assisted in the house, cleaned and cooked for her parents, but was excused from doing the shopping and thus exposing herself to stares and taunts. One evening when she was washing the dishes, her mother came into the kitchen. She began to wipe the glasses and dishes in the drainer but stopped, towel in hand, and stared into the small kitchen garden behind the washhouse where her father grew vegetables and cabbage. It had come in handy, whatever he'd been able to grow in the small strip of land, while there was a shortage of everything. "Who would've thought my daughter to end up a soldier's whore," she said in a low voice, as if speaking to herself. Sigrid didn't answer. "Don't tell me you're waiting," her mother continued, a little louder. "You're not fancying that the German pig was in love with you?" Sigrid turned toward her. She had accustomed herself from when she was little to seeing only faint and indirect traces of whatever her mother felt on her coarse, contracted face, and she'd never before witnessed or even pictured to herself that it might actually shine with evil. Her mother's words repeated themselves in her head when she had gone to bed, like a record stuck in the same groove.

As weeks and months passed, she lost her faith that a letter from Thomas would finally arrive, or that he would come back as he had promised. To begin with, she told herself that of course he couldn't come, the situation being what it was in his country. She kept fighting back the thought that he had made a fool of her, and that she had loved him in vain. She never surrendered to that thought.

"I suppose he forgot you," I said harshly when she had told me her story. She shook her head. "Oh, no," she said softly, "that would make no sense."

I have moved, Anna. I live on Amerikavej again, and there is such a childish crudeness to my joy that it hardly fits into my septuagenarian frame. I almost didn't bring anything. I emailed the boys and told them they could come and take whatever they wanted. Stefan never answered; he is sore. Morten came in a rental van to collect the Kjaerholm sofa. This way, he wouldn't have to invest in the sofa Mie recommended to him, I thought, but I didn't say anything. He made sure to avoid speaking of her or Stefan, and I inferred that they must have talked about our failed tête-à-tête.

I remember when you got your new sofa, you and Georg. You invited us to come over for the inauguration, and Henning couldn't stop caressing the brandy-colored calfskin. The first many times I sat in it, it felt like being on probation. You know the feeling I always had, of not being good enough. You knew it, but you didn't know the reason why I felt ashamed. I still do from time to time, although I have put it all behind me, like the furniture. I called an Internet auction house and had them collect the rest. Afterward, I went to IKEA and found the most basic stuff — a bed, a table, a few chairs. It's a little less than empty here. Can you say such a thing, Anna? Below empty, meaning sparsely furnished. They say it's trendy, by the way. Less than nothing, meaning not dead yet. With a little luck, and if I have the brains for it, I may have fifteen, perhaps twenty years left. Not bad when you think about it, but I have no time for nonsense. I have no time for Stefan and his self-centered way of feeling rejected.

I hadn't heard from him in weeks when he suddenly called. Why had I never answered? I told him I had canceled the landline phone. But I didn't answer my cell phone, either, he insisted. I explained to him that it hadn't been charged since Georg died. But I answered now! Was it because he called from a different number? I hadn't even looked at the digits on the display. He had called and called. His tone was oscillating between offended and reproachful. I tried to tell him that my phone has an unfortunate tendency to go into soundless mode, without my having asked it. You've been spared a lot, Anna, where those things are concerned. Cell phones lead their own lives, or rather, we live theirs. Cordless, oh yes, but always available. What kind of freedom is that? Of course I could have decided not to answer it.

I was in a discount DIY in the western suburbs, speculating if I had room for ten liters of wall paint in my handlebar basket, or if I should make do with five. They were hefty tubs, I tell you, but there is something pleasurable about doing things yourself. Getting lost in the routines of the job. I am beginning to understand why Georg loved his workbench in the garage so much.

Everything was in its place on the shelves. He had even outlined the claw hammer and the crowbar and whatnot with a pencil on the perforated Masonite sheet where he hung his tools. When I saw it for the first time, I almost said something witty, but I kept my mouth shut. Stefan loved to stand out there with him and be let in on it, contrary to Morten, who shunned implements of all kinds, as if they were evil creatures out to bite and scratch him. He sprawled on the Kjaerholm sofa reading Enid Blyton while Stefan and Georg were fixing things. There is historic justice to the fact that the sofa has become his and Thea's, but it isn't what it used to be, I have to confess that, Anna. First, there is the cup of cocoa that was spilled during I don't know which birthday party, and the cushions have become chappy. I should have thought to wax them. Do you remember how you rubbed away?

Stefan had an agenda, I could hear that as I wavered between luster 10 and luster 20. He was angry, and his anger had been accumulating. He had been compelled to deposit it at the bank, so to speak, since he couldn't get through to me on the cell or the landline phone, and now it was payback time, with interest. He demanded that I apologize. "What for?" I asked. "You are to excuse yourself to Mie. You are to treat my wife with dignity." He had a comically solemn way of saying "my wife," as if we were strangers. Suddenly we were. My voice was thick with uneasiness. "I think I do," I said. "You have no right to cast aspersions on her motherhood," he persisted. Oh, I thought to myself, of course. Stefan is a good, empathic husband. He has

83

been sent on an errand. "You don't even know what you're talking about; you never tried it yourself," he continued. Bloodlust, I thought, and felt myself becoming tough and cold. "That might be," I said, "but I still don't believe it's healthy for children to be breast-fed until they change their teeth. They may get some antibodies on that account, but they will be lacking in backbone if they're not weaned in time. They were about to gnaw off her nipples." He was silent for a moment. His voice sounded completely different when he continued mutedly: "I had no idea that you could be so base," he said. "And yet, I guess I knew all along."

I remained standing with my phone after he had hung up. I remembered again his tiddly, infantile way of blabbering about tits when he'd had a little too much red wine, ebulliently self-satisfied in the role of bad boy. It was useless since there would never be an opportunity to remind him about it. In any event, his ears were incapable of tuning in to any other wavelength than Mie's. I guess he's the dream of a husband, brutally fixated on his career yet biddable at home. As I lugged the bucket of paint out to my bike, I realized that he had touched me on the raw. He had known where to strike. He'd had that knowledge in reserve throughout without betraying it, and I'd never given it a thought. The humiliation etched itself into where he had intended it to catch up with me as I biked back into town. It is an awkward business, to balance ten liters of emulsion paint in your handlebar basket when you feel as exposed as that. As if everybody can see the kind of person you are. It wasn't that I'd never known the prototypical, estrogenic fermentation of motherhood, God bless. Where that was concerned I was only baffled, slightly dizzy even, at Stefan's determination to go all the way, but his final remark went further. The word *base*. His admission that he'd never forgotten, never entirely disregarded where I really came from. He had struck a hideous, grimy bottom within me, and it was no solace that he knew nothing about the even deeper shaft beneath it.

Sigrid's vague ideas of something more never got her very far. An avalanche came in the way, and suddenly she was somewhere else. It was midwinter when she gave birth to me at the hospital in Naestved. One of her mother's elder cousins lived in that town and let Sigrid move in shortly before her delivery. The story was to go that my father was a sailor on a coaster. I was told a version of it when I was five years old and began to ask questions. In it, his ship had gone down after hitting a mine. The cousin shook her head in place of condemnation. "My dear," she said, "what a mess you've gotten yourself mixed up in." She bought accessories for her, including romper suits and cotton diapers, and she lent her an old stroller that had been left over in the basement. One evening, a week after my birth, Sigrid boarded the last bus back to Stege. The driver helped her with the stroller. His kindness brought tears to her eyes because she thought of what was coming to her. Even though she had made sure to arrive when most people were going to bed, it still felt as if she were being watched from the windows as she passed. The dark, glossy windowpanes reflected the streetlights, and behind them she imagined how they watched as the German-loving slut returned with her progeny.

She had made her decision before she reached her parents' door. Her mother must have thought likewise. The next day, she went to the savings bank and withdrew the full amount on her checkbook. She put the banknotes on the oilcloth in front of Sigrid. Her father sat wheezing in the living room. "It was supposed to sweeten our old age," her mother said, "but take it. Take it and go away." They never saw each other again. The following evening, Sigrid boarded yet another late-night bus and put us up at the railway hotel in Vordingborg. As she went to sleep in the unfamiliar room, she must have thought that now Thomas wouldn't be able to find her, should he finally come one day. The morning after, she took the train to Copenhagen. Many people were helpful toward the young woman traveling alone with a baby, a stroller, and a suitcase.

She had enough money to move into a modest boardinghouse for a start. Being a lonely mother she soon got me into a day nursery, and she started looking for a job. She was hired by a cardboard factory in Vanlose, and soon after that she was lucky enough to get the apartment on Amerikavej, but her workdays were long, and she was overwhelmed by the fatigues of biking to and fro, summer and winter, returning just in time to fetch me. Instead, she had various jobs and places until she resigned herself at last to cleaning at a school when the children had gone home. It was tiresome but manageable, and a woman in our house was kind and looked after me until I was old enough to be alone.

Sigrid exchanged Christmas cards with her mother's cousin in Naestved, and she thought that if Thomas would try one day to get in touch with her, he would probably be referred to the cousin. It was through her that she received the news of her father's death. Years later the Christmas cards stopped, meaning the cousin must also be dead, and after still more years, she figured out that the same thing must apply to her mother. When I look back on that period, I always remind myself that the loneliness, the hardships, and the recurrent thoughts of my father must partially have been made up for by the relief that nobody knew anything. Her loneliness was like a tundra. During the first years after the war, she must have told herself that she didn't deserve the kindness that was occasionally shown to her. She must have felt like an impostor. When I had become a big girl, and she told me who my father was, she consigned me to the same solitude. We couldn't even support one another. You are always alone with your shame, and it makes you almost hate the one you love.

I was a mistake; I should never have been born. In the mind of my younger self, my mother's love story could never outweigh the story of her disgrace. It was mine, too, and it has followed me all these years like a stubborn stray dog. No one has ever been more faithful than my scurvy mutt, and no one knows me better. One day I heard the greengrocer tell a customer what should have been done to my kind back then. It was in the blood, he said. I lowered my eyes, and my mouth ran dry as I waited for my turn. I thought about it constantly, beneath my other thoughts and everything that passed. I was always watchful. I had to make an effort so that no one would notice anything. "Ellinor is always so happy," one of my teachers once said to my mother. My hypocrisy came off on everything, even on my joy. If someone would say something nice or just be dear to me, I couldn't allow myself to take it in. It wasn't me, after all. I wasn't the person they thought I was. I was someone else, the bastard of the German-loving slut.

It wasn't that she had spread her legs to the enemy. Thomas Hoffmann had been no Nazi, and it was a handsome man my mother had told me about in a hushed voice, as if others were listening. As if she wanted to excuse herself. My spontaneous reaction was to become irritated. In the days that followed, I thought that it seemed as if I had known it always. I had never had many friends; my natural inclination had been to isolate myself, like Sigrid. Had others not avoided me without my noticing it? Could they see it in my face that my father was German? I stood in front of the mirror, scrutinizing myself. She had said that I looked like him. I tried to extract the features that were not hers, the afterimage of an unknown.

No, of course he had been no Nazi monster. It was loneliness itself that was shameful. The secret stuck to us like an unwanted odor, the ever-lurching fear of being found out, recognized, pointed at. Vesterbro and the shabby modesty of it all was a cover, and we also lost track of each other. I avoided taking friends home with me and took refuge wherever I was invited. I felt miserable when I warmed myself at the cheerfulness of an ordinary family. If I spent the night at a friend's place, I couldn't fall asleep for fear of giving myself away while I was dreaming. I lay awake in the unfamiliar apartment, alone in the world, yet relieved to be away from home. I dreamed of disappearing. When I became a grown-up one day, I would travel far away from my mother and her story. I couldn't tell my guilt from my impatience. I became the kind of girl who doesn't stand out, good at finding my place and blending in. *Opportunistic* is the word, I guess. You arrange yourself with your shame, as you would with some deformity. So did Sigrid; she entrenched herself in it, and it made her haughty.

She almost never saw anyone because she had me to take care of, and the women her age with whom she would sometimes make friends began to have children of their own. I remember her speaking with the other mothers at the playground. She could be easygoing and all smiles, and I think that she enjoyed the chance to sit there and be like one of them. As if she had a husband who would come home from work, and parents we could see on Sundays. In fact, there was no need for her to remain lonely. She was only in her middle twenties when I started in the first grade. In the third grade, I remember that we were called on by a man named Ejgil. He must have been fifteen years her senior, a silent, balding, blond man who smoked cigarettes. His wife had died of cancer; they had had no children. "As good luck would have it," my mother once said. Ejgil was a woodworking teacher at the school where my mother cleaned. They had met one day when he was tidying the woodworking room. Two lonely figures in the empty, silent school.

After a few weeks, my mother invited him to come and eat with us since he was alone anyway. That was how she justified his presence in advance the first time he was coming. The widower who came for a meal, as though he wouldn't otherwise eat. He would come a couple of times every week. He always brought me something, a sachet of sweets, a bar of chocolate. My mother said he wasn't to spoil me, but he just smiled. Sometimes he would read me a bedtime story while my mother was in the kitchen doing the dishes, and I thought that this must be what it was like in my classmates' homes. I heard the two of them from my bed, talking quietly in the living room. On Sundays, he invited us to the zoo or to the movies, and once we went to Bakken. We took a horse cab from the station, through the forest, and he looked as if he was just as excited as I was. I got used to walking hand in hand with him; his hand was large and warm and firm. He put together a dollhouse for me and made small furniture for it and bought me dolls. Stiff little people who sat, legs outstretched, on his fine little chairs. I never played with that house, but I still have it.

That summer, I was going to a camp on Bornholm. I'd never seen rocks before. I didn't know the other children, and it made me feel free since we all had the same grown-ups around us, whether we had a mom and a dad at home or not. One of the first things I asked upon my return was when Ejgil was coming. My mother told me that he wouldn't come anymore. I asked her why. She said that he had moved to another city. I could hear that she was lying, but she didn't seem to be upset about it. "We didn't fit," she added, as if she was aware that I had seen through her. I didn't understand a thing. Four years later, when she had told me the story about Thomas, I asked her again about Ejgil's disappearance. "Did you not want him?" I asked. She shrugged. "Did you not want him because you still loved my father?" Her smile made me blush. "But dearest," she said, "by then it was long ago already."

Morten came on a surprise visit the other day. I was painting the walls of the living room. I finished a section while he was climbing the stairs. He stopped in the doorway and smiled approvingly as I turned to him, roller in my hand. "It's going to be nice," he said. "It's going to be white," I answered. "This is a funny neighborhood," he said. I couldn't help smiling. "Do you think it's funny?" He gesticulated. "I mean, colorful." I didn't comment any further. I like Morten. It is my privilege as a stepmother, Anna, now that your boys are long since grown-up men. I am entitled to prefer one to the other, and I can't even bother to make a secret of it. Morten I can talk to, only not about Vesterbro. He will always be a boy from the suburbs. Funny. Colorful. Seedy. Horrifying. He didn't understand what his stepmother was doing among African hairdressers and girls in thigh-length platform boots. He said that he had some papers from the attorney for me to sign. He didn't mention that it was of course Stefan who had sent him. Papers from an attorney have never been Morten's field. We went into the adjoining room. He didn't rise when I had signed in the places marked by the attorney's secretary with small yellow vanes. He asked if I would offer him a cup of coffee. "Of course," I said, apologizing all the way into the kitchen. Forty years of training, Anna, and I hadn't even asked your son if he could use a cup of tea or coffee.

He could use someone to talk to. It was still about his colleague at the university, his fling from last autumn. To begin with, he seemed ill at ease, not just over his colleague but also from just talking about her. After all, we were still mourning his father, and wasn't that more important? I took his hand and squeezed it shortly. "We can talk about her if you want to," I said. I could see from his face that he understood that I understood, and he soon found his tongue. It was weird to pass each other every day as faculty. She behaved toward him like she had before the affair, almost, that is; perhaps a bit more reservedly. As if it had never happened. They had met every afternoon in the apartment of a friend of his while the friend was away. It had been strong stuff to meet her on campus and make as if nothing was going on, knowing that a few hours later they would be in bed, embracing. I asked myself if he would have talked to me about his affair in that way if I had been his mother.

"And then your friend came back?" I said. "She broke it off before that," he answered gravely. "So she didn't want to leave her husband after all?" I said. "She wasn't ready," Morten said. "She needed more time. She needed me to respect that she was at a loss. She told me not to push her." He sighed. "Did you push her?" I asked. "She said that she felt torn at seeing how miserable I was, and because Masja had kicked me out." He gathered the papers from the attorney in a pile. "Do you think that Masja might take you back?" I asked. "Never," he said. "And I don't want to go back. I don't ever want to feel so . . ." He stopped in the middle of the sentence, searching for the right word. "Torn?" I asked. "Yes," he said, and he seemed not to notice the smile on my face. "Doesn't it make you feel even more torn to stand between two women who don't want you?" He looked at me. "But that's it," he said. "That's why Agnete feels that she's under pressure. She tells me that she can't make a decision as long as I'm . . . as long as she is feeling guilty because . . ." I lifted the coffeepot. "Do you want some more?" He handed me his cup. "So poor, torn Agnete can't bring herself to perhaps leave her husband until you relieve her by recovering from your infatuation?"

He couldn't help smiling, either. We sat for a while without saying anything. He looked at the pile of documents in front of him. "May I ask you something?" he said. "Go ahead," I replied. "The money you spent on the apartment . . . Of course it's none of my business . . ." I put my hand flat on the papers. "Since Stefan knows, you have a right to know as well. My first

93

husband, Henning, who died at the same time as your mother . . ." I locked his gaze with mine and made an effort not to blink. I had suddenly realized that we'd never talked about your death. Isn't that strange, Anna? Georg must have talked about it with the boys when they grew older, but not when I was around, and I'm sure that he never betrayed you. It would have hurt them; it would have disturbed the trifling memory you'd left behind. "Henning's mother had no heirs," I continued, "and she left me some money I've never spent." He nodded. "But why did it have to be a secret?" he asked. "Did Stefan say it was?" I asked. "No, no," he said. For a moment I considered telling him everything, but I didn't.

You can trust me, Anna, as you can trust Georg. The twins know nothing about you and Henning. You were just friends. I hadn't talked to his mother for a long time when I heard that she'd died. I would have liked to visit her in the hospital, and my conscience didn't improve when I got a letter from an attorney telling me that I was her sole heir. I asked Georg to open an account for me and just leave the money like that. I believe he sensed that I was disturbed by the mere thought of it, and we never discussed the matter again. I had almost forgotten about it.

When Morten had gone, I resumed painting. The roller sounded like car tires on a street in the rain. I always loved that sound; it epitomizes the city for me. I have always loved the city, Anna, including while I was living in your home, leading your life. I was never a suburbanite like yourself and your children. From time to time, I saw my chance to take the S-train into town. Georg didn't know, and I always made sure to be back when the twins came home from school. I had stopped working, you see. I started again only when the boys began grammar school. My former boss had long since retired, and there were no classifieds anymore, but I was hired as a proofreader. That way, I got to read the newspaper every day. I know the words, Anna. I know them from my rainy afternoons on Amerikavej when I opened the dictionary at random or simply followed the alphabet. But I took care of your house and your boys and your husband for years, and I almost felt that it was mine, that they were mine. While other women rebelled and swarmed into the job market, I went about the premises, shopping and cooking. I escorted the boys to their soccer training, I had a grip on birthdays and homework, and I wasn't bored. In a strange way, I felt free, liberated.

It goes without saying that I spent a good part of the day on my own. At times, when I had finished something and didn't yet have to throw myself into the next task, I would lie down on the floor in the living room. I lay on my back between the furniture with my eyes closed. I listened to the few sounds penetrating the wide, double-glazed windows overlooking the terrace: a bird, leaves in the wind, a car driving by. The soft rustle from a radiator. My father doesn't know that I exist, I thought. Nobody knows that he doesn't know.

At other times I went into town, as I said. It came over me every now and then. I walked about at random from one neighborhood to the next. If it started raining, I would simply button up my coat and allow my hair to become wet. It always dries again, Anna. There isn't a thing that doesn't pass off. It strikes me that my account must seem sad to you, but I am not a sad person, and you know that. Often I am happy, as the song goes, happy inside, even if I can't always show it. It is all just something that passes you by. You're being pushed and pressed, sometimes even crushed, and you can be knocked off your course, but you remain the same on the inside. You grow older and the city changes, but they are the same eyes and the same streets. I had followed the same routes when I was a big girl. During the years from when I was confirmed until I moved in with the widow on Søndre Fasanvej, I liked to roam on my own. I didn't want to sit at home with my mother or be there when she came back from work. It wasn't that Sigrid was a tough mother, on the contrary, and if I wanted her not to disturb me, all I had to do was read. I read all of her books, and when I'd read the last one, I moved. I read or went for a walk when there wasn't anything I had to do, through the narrow streets in the Latin Quarter or far out into Frederiksberg.

Once, I stopped in front of a gateway on Smallegade because there was such a lovely smell of glue and freshly planed wood. There was a small cabinetmaker's workshop in the back building; one could just see the dark-green machines under the strip lights. A woman appeared in the courtyard, wheeling a bike, and I was about to continue when I stopped again, recognizing the voice that spoke to her. The woman waited until he caught up with her. Two merging silhouettes in the gateway, assuming their features and colors again as they came out into the gray light. Ejgil hadn't changed at all, and he also recognized me. The woman eyed me watchfully as we greeted one another. She wore a scarf tied under her chin, setting off her round cheeks. She must be my mother's age, perhaps younger. "This is Vibeke," he said. I shook her hand and made a flurried curtsy. "My, how you've grown," he said and smiled, "but I guess they tell you so all the time." I smiled back and shrugged. "I still have the dollhouse," I said. "Do you?" His eyes began to wander. "Well, we're off. Say hello, will you?" I turned around on the sidewalk to look at them as they continued in the opposite direction. He wheeled her bike for her, and she held his arm.

Perhaps, I thought, as I continued past Lorry and the small gardens, perhaps my mother spoke the truth. Maybe she was never at a loss; maybe she never felt torn between the memory of a young German officer who read Ibsen and a not-so-young woodworking teacher who had taken the time to make a dollhouse for her daughter. Could it be that it was really such a long time ago, and she had naturally abandoned the idea that, like the sailor in *The Lady from the Sea*, her officer might one day return and take her with him? That he might return, after all those years, so that it would have made sense, all of it, the longing, the shame, and the loneliness? But if she had taken Ejgil, and my father had come one day, and Ejgil had set her free, gentle and magnanimous, would she then have chosen her woodworking teacher in preference to the officer who had let her wait for so long? If she wasn't torn by an impossible dream, what, then, had kept her back?

As the years passed, something hard came over Sigrid, and I think that she alienated people, possibly without knowing it herself. If I asked her why she never saw anyone, she would answer that she preferred reading to prattling. "What would I want a mangler for when I can talk with Dostoyevsky?" she asked, visibly satisfied with her reply. Or a woodworking teacher, I thought. She had always had her books, even before the story with Thomas Hoffmann. Her books and her ideas, however vague, of something more.

I wonder if Henning ever got around to feeling torn. How long did it last, your secret life before the avalanche? Did the guilt have time to tear at you, or was it all adventure and lightness at stepping through an invisible wall, into a world different from the one you'd known? A different, impossible version that you probably hadn't even fantasized about. Another mouth, another pair of eyes, other hands. A different smell. The adventurous lightness when the unexpected happens, and you feel that you yourself could be someone else, free at last.

You were that lightness, Anna. I understand him. I could talk with him, and we could daydream together, but even though I was far from being the glum kind, he could feel very well how my inside and my outside personas were seldom in phase. I understand him, I really do. I've also warmed myself in front of you. When he found me and brought me along for chestnuts and red wine with someone called Georg and Anna, I was still this perished little creature, dumped out of a gray past not even worth bidding farewell. You seized every occasion for parties and happy commotion; you always found something to laugh about. Of course he must have fallen in love with you from the very first second, without knowing. You almost didn't have to do anything to remind him, and perhaps it simply started as one of your sudden impulses. You were unable to pass a plum tree in September without having to taste what it had to offer. You have meant no harm, I am certain of that, and it never occurred to you that you were taking something that belonged to me. You hadn't given the future a single thought as your moment spread. One would say that you had a better sense than I had of life's opportunities. You simply had to feel with your own hands, your own lips, how possible life can be. *Easygoing*, that's the word for it, and I felt it when I stepped into your place. Oh, yes, I said to myself, to think that life can be this inviting, even on a Monday. It felt like stepping through that invisible wall.

We were terribly modest to begin with. We had to turn off the lights and pretend to be somebody else. They are the same motions, the same elevated wrestling, no matter who we are. As if we are mere links, for the duration of that moment, body-to-body, in mankind's long chain of desire and reproduction, as in the Indian temple reliefs where they copulate in all directions in teeming, filigree-like eternity. In daylight, there were Ellinor and Georg, strange enough as it was; and in the darkness, there were two unfamiliar bodies falling into the primeval routine, relieved that we were at least not as alien as our bodies. Ultimately, anyone can screw anyone; only when faces are added does it become a story about something more than that. And faces were added in due course. I understood what it was about his calm that must have felt like a safe cave, and yet I didn't understand you at all. Was it important that he was older than you, while Henning was your age? I had been mystified at the beginning as to what you had seen in Georg, but later on the mystery was how you could ever have preferred flighty Henning to the safety of Georg's grip. Taking your place didn't mean that I understood you any better. I love you, Anna, and I've never understood you. I don't know what else would have become of me. It's a terrible thing to say, but I have a lot to thank you for.

Of course Georg talked to the boys before I moved in. He came over to inform me of the outcome of their negotiations. Your father had taken them to a soccer match as usual. In the meantime, I had removed every trace of Henning, and the apartment looked as if it had always been the home of a single woman. They had taken it the way boys take those things, fairly aloof. They had asked where I was supposed to sleep but didn't comment on the answer. We were in the house, both of us, when they came back. It was helpful, I am sure, that your father was just as happy to see me as he used to be. The first evening was awkward, but it soon wore off. During the following days, I gave them to understand by way of little remarks that I wasn't intending to make them forget about you or that they needed to stop themselves when they were unhappy. We talked about you every evening, and they told me stories from your vacations. It really felt as if you were sitting somewhere, listening. Like a bird on a twig, you sat, now here, now there, in my mind's ramification of remembered moments.

You were part of our everyday life, and you were quoted frequently. The boys were very helpful and informative at the beginning, when I stood in the kitchen in the morning, preparing their lunch boxes, or when they came home in the afternoon with a troop of noisy classmates. It surprised me how much they were usually allowed to do. You wouldn't have approved of it all, Anna, but what was I supposed to do? Only after a couple of years did I begin to impose my own rules, as Georg and I had to tackle the tribulations and temptations of a new age level. I improved my grasp, even when things became critical, and I discovered that they had begun to trust me. Belatedly, I realized that they liked me. This wasn't something they would advertise and yet I received, drop by drop, some of the love in which Georg was basking. We struck a cheerful, sometimes playful note that came to resonate with all the things you never say. I think I would have been a good mother, had I been able.

Georg and I kept sitting and talking in the evening when they had gone to bed. We almost never watched TV during those first years. He talked about his childhood on the farm in Jutland, about his brothers and sisters and about his youth, or he told me what had happened at the office. He was doing well and got promoted all the time. I also told him about my early years, and sometimes I almost told him about Thomas Hoffmann. It wasn't that I didn't trust him. I was certain that he would have felt nothing but sympathy for Sigrid and me. I said to myself that it was just an old story from the war. Today, nobody would think of blaming my mother, or condemn her as they had back when she was expelled and she herself withdrew in disgrace and isolation. Still, I never said anything. It may have been the thought of his compassion that made me keep silent, and in time it became too late. As I got to know him better, I understood that it would have hurt him that I hadn't told him the story early on.

As time went by we didn't talk that often about Henning and you, or about what had happened in the Dolomites when we were young. We got friends of our own whom you'd never known; we got ourselves a life. Little by little, our story became longer than yours and Georg's had been. We belonged together.

He made an effort to include my mother. She would often come to dinner on Sundays, she and your parents took turns looking after the boys when we were going out, and she was a fixture for Christmas. The first couple of years, we celebrated Christmas with all of the grandparents until Georg's father and mother became too old to make the trip. I was surprised at my mother; she was lively and courteous, and it dawned on me that I'd never seen her in the company of more than one or two at a time. Nobody would have guessed that she was the daughter of a worker from Stege, just as nobody would have guessed whose daughter I was. There were hard, pointed seconds when I sat in my nice home and felt that we were frauds, my mother and I. The feeling has been there always, but most of the time, it was like a dark fish, barely visible, hiding in the mire under the days' flow of events, doings, and planning. Only every now and then did it come up to gasp for air, during the night, while Georg slept by my side.

I'd never been very affectionate with her. Everything between us had been so tied up when I still lived at home, and in the years after, I neglected to call her or come to visit. She wasn't the one to butt in. She kept to herself, with dignity, until my conscience was too heavy and I came, edgy and short-tempered, already on my way out again. Georg must have noticed. With his example, he taught me to care for her. She came to stay with Stefan and Morten one of the few times he persuaded me to travel with him. It was Easter, and that year, your parents were going to Salerno to see your father's family. Georg found that it would be too much hassle to take the boys to his parents in Jutland, and he asked what I thought. My mother was tremendously honored by his confidence. He fetched her on Amerikavej, so that she wouldn't have to take the S-train with her suitcase. Spring had come early, and we sat on the terrace in the sharp afternoon sunlight. We hadn't been alone together in a long time. Georg and I were taking the night train to Paris a few hours later. "It's a nice life you've got," she said and closed her eyes in the sun. "Yes," I said. On a sudden impulse I reached out for her hand, hanging limply from the armrest of her deck chair. I almost had second thoughts about it, but I did it anyway, and I felt her fingers as they closed around mine.

She fell ill a couple of years later, and after a long period of surgery, treatments, hope, and relapses, it suddenly went fast. I came to see her in the hospital every day. She told me things she'd never talked about before. After I moved in with the widow on Søndre Fasanvej, she had known various men. She enjoyed how baffled I was. It had never lasted very long, but they had been more than just a few. It amused her to enumerate their merits and flaws, and how different they'd been. There was something almost frivolous about her as she talked, and I was surprised to see her like that, but why not go for it when someone showed an interest? In my thoughts, I argued that it was her merriment that made me feel nettled. But why? She never mentioned my father and soon became too weakened to speak for more than a few minutes. One of the last times I saw her, I asked if she had never considered finding out what had become of him. She lay with her eyes closed, dozing off already because of the medicine. She resembled an old woman, although she wasn't even sixty. I thought that she'd fallen asleep when she suddenly lifted a hand and gestured, mumbling something I couldn't understand.

I came back the next day, but she slept most of the time. They called from the ward during the evening. Georg answered the phone. When we got there it was too late. The nurse had folded her hands. She looked as though she was just sleeping. Georg put his arms around me, and I hid my face at his chest. I couldn't tell him how relieved I was.

I miss him, my husband, our husband; I miss him so. There are times when I don't know what to do with myself. That's when I think that I've made a big mistake moving to Amerikavej. He would never find me here if he were to come back. I am not insane. It has dawned on me that human beings were never meant to reconcile their longing with reason, not at the expense of longing. As if I could love him in a lesser way just because he's dead. That was never the meaning of words. That is why I am speaking to you.

There are times when I cannot hold his absence, and the feeling is a physical one, Anna; it is not a metaphor. Then I walk the streets like I did when I was a big girl and later, when I was the stepmother of your sons out there in my self-chosen exile. Anna, I've promised myself that I'll never see a carport again. I walk at random through the city, following my impulse or something that catches my eye. I forget myself as I walk; I am only these eyes in the same streets as before. Sometimes I go into the Latin Quarter to stroll around in the old alleys, or I walk to the end of Frederiksberg and farther, all the way to Vanløse. I have tried to find the cardboard factory where Sigrid found herself a job when she came to town, but I think it's been demolished.

You sit like a bird in my mind's ramification, and sometimes you flap your wings, take off, and settle somewhere else. There is something you want to ask me about, I know. You want me to tell you why I never tried to find out whatever became of my father. Those things are possible today — they even make TV shows about it. Nothing is more successful in prime time than a choked reunion, but who knows if he would have been happy to see me? He had no inkling of my existence. But that's exactly it, you will say. How have I been able to live with it? His never knowing?

You don't understand. After a few years, I realized what I think my mother tried to say with her vague gesture and her mumbling voice, dulled by the medicine. It was all the same. He could have come after the war if he wasn't already dead at that point. He didn't come, whether he was dead or he had forgotten her or he just wanted to do something else, and it was all the same if he didn't come of himself. If he didn't come because he wanted to, it didn't matter to her whether he was still alive. I believe that's how my mother thought. I ascribe such pride to her, but I also ascribe such defenseless trust.

When I moved in with Georg and the boys, I had the picture framed of the two of you dancing a slowfox a few years before we met. I hung it on the wall in their room, so that they could see how much their parents had loved each other. It's the only thing that counts for a child. We forgive our parents when they forget us, if only they love each other. I think about it every time I try to see Thomas Hoffmann, that late summer when he walked with my mother under the harvest moon, out at the cove.

Other titles published by Ulverscroft:

HAPPIEST DAYS

Jack Sheffield

It's 1986, and Jack Sheffield returns to Ragley village school for his tenth rollercoaster year as headteacher. It's the time of Margaret Thatcher's third election victory, *Dynasty* and shoulder pads, *Neighbours* and a Transformer for Christmas. And at Ragley School, a year of surprises is in store. Ruby the caretaker finds happiness at last, Vera the secretary makes an important decision, a new teacher is appointed, and a disaster threatens the school. Meanwhile, Jack receives unexpected news, and is faced with the biggest decision of his career . . .

LITTLE BEACH STREET BAKERY

Jenny Colgan

Amid the ruins of her latest relationship, Polly Waterford moves far away to the sleepy seaside resort of Mount Polbearne, where she lives in a small, lonely flat above an abandoned shop. To distract her from her troubles, Polly throws herself into her favourite hobby: making bread. But her relaxing weekend diversion quickly develops into a passion. As she pours her emotions into kneading and pounding the dough, each loaf becomes better than the last. Soon, Polly is working her magic with nuts and seeds, olives and chorizo, and honey — courtesy of a handsome local beekeeper. Drawing on reserves of determination and creativity Polly never knew she had, she bakes and bakes . . . and discovers a bright new life where she least expected it.